# HIGH HEELS AND COWBOY BOOTS

## A LONE TREE RANCH ROMANCE

## DAWN LUEDECKE

D1713679

ABOUT THIS BOOK

**Will Jax finally get a second chance with the girl who stole his truck and his heart?**

The last thing Jax McCall wants is a second chance at romance, especially with Emmy Wilson. She broke his heart in high school, stranded him on a mountainside, and now she's a contestant in a film project hosted at his ranch. As much as Jax should keep things all business with Emmy, he can't get her out of his mind.

Emmy Wilson has a famous mother and famous cowboy father. She wants nothing more than to succeed on her own and this assignment can do that for her. Except the familiar cowboy who picks her up at the airport could ruin everything, especially when he looks at her like he knows even her deepest secrets.

*To Katherine York. Thank you for being an awesome friend. Let's do this series!*

Cover Model Images by Period Images and Pi Creative Lab.

Background image by DepositPhotos.

Cover Text, Logo, and Branding by Christina Hovland.

Proofread/Edited by: Britaini Armitage

A LONE TREE RANCH ROMANCE

"Well written, well researched. Like the river, this plot runs faster and faster. Readers won't be able to put it down."

**—New York Times bestselling author Jodi Thomas on WHITE WATER PASSION**

I am so glad a friend recommended this book. This was amazingly awesome. And wow look at that cover. I was intrigued from the first page. I couldn't wait to see how the story was going to unfold. Truly I say I will end up reading this book definitely several more times. I'm so glad there are more books by this author.

**— -REVIEWER ON HARD TO LOVE**

If you read my review of the first book in this series, you will know that I absolutely loved it. The same goes for this novel, Wild Passion. I stayed up until 4am on a Saturday night to finish this book.

**— -LASR REVIEWS ON WILD PASSION**

This book affected me in a way no other book has. I just finished reading White Water Passion and I feel emotionally and physically exhausted yet I feel like I just won something grand. I can't even compare this feeling to anything in my personal life but I feel like I just participated in a river drive; as if I just survived riding a log down the wild rapids. I couldn't wait to write the review for fear I'd lose this feeling that I have which is a feeling of amazing victory. There were so many unpredictable plot twists that were so suspenseful, I couldn't read nor turn the pages fast enough. It's amazing how I was sucked into the events in this story. Seriously, if I hear a twig snap behind me then I'm going to expect Garrett to save me.

## CHAPTER 1

"Did you see the latest?" Vivian slammed a magazine down on Emmy Wilson's desk, the binding bent to reveal yet another photo of Stacy Siepres with all her lady parts on display for the world. "The girl wore a miniskirt and crotchless panties to her own concert. She's either a true artist or a rebelling twenty-something-year-old trying to prove how insane she is to the world."

"Oh, she's bat-shit crazy, but either way she's a gold mine for us." Emmy ran a quick critical eye over the article, stopping at the blurred X-rated picture of her childhood neighbor, Stacy. "She must be cold. Her nipples are poking through her pasties."

"I'm not one to judge anyone's lifestyle, but this chick takes it to the limit." Viv leaned over her shoulder and studied the picture. "I don't think those are pasties."

"Well, when you're famous, you can test any boundary you want." Emmy knew from experience. That's how her movie star mother had lived her life. Emmy mimicked her boss' move and brought the magazine close to her face to study the picture. "Definitely not pasties. Is that body paint?"

"Probably." Vivian sat on Emmy's desk and folded her arms across her chest. "*The Click* got this scoop first."

"What we need is a new, better story." Emmy's chair squeaked when she leaned back. The damned thing needed greasing. She made a mental note to let the janitor know later. "We need a story that gets us inside that twisted mind of hers and blows *The Click* and all our other competitors out of the water. Do you want me to put Candice on the story?"

"Nope." Vivian gave Emmy her *I've got something you're not going to like* smile.

"What?" Emmy's heart palpitated. The look on Viv's face never bode good for anyone on the receiving end of the smile.

"She's doing some promo shots for a show she's producing or something. She wants to give you the exclusive."

"Me? But I'm just your assistant." Plus, she had no intention of reconnecting with Stacy. She knew too much about her past, and the last thing she wanted was for her free-loving, old neighbor to run her mouth and expose something she shouldn't.

"You've got something special," Vivian continued, "and we need that."

"What? A Masters Degree? A lot of people here have that."

"Besides the fact that she requested you specifically, I didn't pluck you out of New York University for nothing. Do this for me, and maybe there will be another field job waiting for you when you get home."

A part of her wanted to jump for joy, but the other wanted to run straight into the women's bathroom and lock the stall door. This was her first story, her breakthrough into real journalism, but she had a funny feeling deep in her gut that it wasn't as it seemed. "Are you sure I'm ready? I had planned to ease my way into this whole job thing. I wouldn't even know where to begin." Okay, that was a lie. She knew exactly where her life was going to go, and she would forge it alone. She just hadn't expected her big break to happen this soon without a little help from her parents. She was now a twenty-seven-year-old college graduate. A self-sufficient woman with a past no one in her professional life would ever know about. Just as long as she kept her past behind her.

Stacy and this job made that difficult.

Viv smiled as if she'd already won. "You can start by saying yes and then going home for the rest of the day. Call your mother, and then pack your stuff."

"What?" *Damn it!* She knew. She had to. Emmy resisted the urge to toss out a few cuss words. There it was. Her mother—the hook and sinker. Keyword sinker. Sometimes she wished she wasn't a part of her life. But you can't help who your family is.

Emmy studied the blank expression pasted to Vivian's face. Did she really know, or was it all a coincidence? When Viv's expression didn't change, Emmy sighed. "What's the show? Vibrato? Acapella Challenge? Or some other singing thing. I'm not as good as my mother, but I can hold a tune enough to get on one of those things."

Vivian sat still with her arms over her chest and let her talk away. Which, in Emmy's experience with her so far, was another sign of bad news. Why do people do that? Sit there with smug looks on their face and let you prattle on, knowing they have more bad news for you. "For Pete sakes, Viv, what is the show?"

"It's called High Heels or Cowboy Boots, so pack both." She plopped a thick manila envelope on Emmy's desk-sized calendar.

"A cowboy show?" Emmy relaxed into her seat. She peeked into the envelope to find a plane ticket and Viv's standard pre-assignment packet, a packet Emmy usually had to type up.

Vivian's chin length hair flipped when she nodded.

"But my mom is Rochelle Wilson," she said, dryly.

"And you're Tye Traver's goddaughter. Three-time NFR saddle bronc champion."

Emmy's heart beat hard in her chest and she grew dizzy. Tye wasn't her godfather. Tye was her dad, but no one knew that secret. Except Stacy Siepres. Not even her mother's agent knew who Emmy's father really was. She didn't expect Viv to know about that part of her past, or at least she hoped she didn't find out. "How did you know?"

Viv's eyes lit up. "It's my job to know."

"You haven't told anyone, have you? We try to keep my godfather's identity a secret. Protect his privacy."

"I was wondering why you hadn't told me. And of course that's the reason I'm letting you go. Do you know any other writer whose mother is famous, or whose godfather is a famous cowboy, and she's friends with Stacy Siepres?"

"Stacy is not my friend. She was my neighbor." Okay, that wasn't exactly the truth. She had been friends with Stacy whenever she was at her mother's house, but that was out of sheer need for social interaction with kids her own age. That was when she was a pre-teen, and they'd long since parted ways.

Viv waved off her comment like there was a fly buzzing in front of her nose. "I think she is trying to make a show about people like you competing against cowboys for things like rodeo and ballroom dancing or something. Like I said, it's just the first couple episodes that they're shooting now. You're the perfect person for this story, and you have an in, so buckle up. You will be in the middle of nowhere Montana and you leave in the morning."

"Wait. What story am I looking for here? The show? Bad girl behavior like in *The Click*? What?"

"Whatever she gives you, just make it juicy." Vivian tossed over her shoulder. "And don't forget to act the part. Keep her close."

"I'll be a raging bimbo," Emmy mumbled. Her heart split in two, and acid churned in her stomach, giving her instant heartburn. If she was going to get through the next few weeks, she would have to be very careful.

Marissa peeked her head around the corner once Viv disappeared into her office. "Is she gone?"

Emmy turned to face her. "Eavesdropping again?"

"I was walking by and heard Viv talking, so I hid." Marissa searched her surroundings and then ducked closer to Emmy. "Why didn't you tell me your mom was a famous actress?"

"Because I don't want anyone in the office to know," she whispered. And she was used to deceiving everyone in her life just to keep her mother's secrets.

"Okay. I won't tell. Promise. Can I just say that I'm super excited to be friends with someone famous?"

"I'm not famous. My mother is." Emmy frowned. "So, are you going to be all weird now?"

"No, but you definitely have to do this story. Imagine... Stacy Siepres."

"Oh, I don't have to imagine." Emmy tossed the magazine across her desk for her friend to see. "Everyone can see every bit of her."

"So, you've had an exciting life, huh?" Marissa peered skyward. "I'll bet you've been to Paris and Rome."

"And Cuba and Zimbabwe, but that's not the point here. I've tried not to let people in the office know about my past for a reason. So let's change the subject before someone overhears."

Marissa's porcelain-skinned, rounded face glistened with

5

an excitement that always meant one thing... shopping. "I'm thinking Bloomingdale's and maybe Saks."

"More like Tractor Warehouse." Emmy turned to her notepad and jotted down the note to the janitor while she spoke.

"No such place in Manhattan. I would have found it by now and gone shopping."

"For a tractor?"

"No. A man buying a tractor. There's nothing like a burley country boy to get the heart pumping, but you probably know all about that."

"True, but unfortunately I will be concentrating on Stacy." Emmy stuffed her information package in her briefcase and shut down her computer. "Wanna play hooky with me for the rest of the day? I need to get packed."

"You had me at play hooky, but why no shopping?"

"No time. Plus, I already have most of what I'll need in my closet."

Marissa sighed. "Fine. I'll just have to go to Tractor Warehouse later by myself. Meet you at my desk in three."

Marissa shut down her computer before Emmy could even gather her things and walk to her cubical. With a half grin, her friend turned and slid her purse strap over her shoulder. "I'm ready, but let's swing by The Bagel Shop. I'm starving."

The next thirty minutes flew by in a whoosh of pushy, self-focused people and New York City cabs—the only thing Emmy hated about the city. It was so different from the easy-going ambiance of the mountain filled air in Montana. Where even the clouds seemed to slow down enough to enjoy the scenery. She missed her life back in the country, but she loved the independence of knowing she was supplying for herself, and not dependent on her parents' fortune to get her by.

After a quick stop at the bagel place next door to her loft so Marissa could get her carb fix, they finally got to Emmy's apartment. She kicked off her pumps, tossed her bag next to the door, and headed toward her room. Holy crap, she hated shoes.

"So what angle are you using for this story?" Marissa asked between bites of her cream cheese smothered bagel.

"Any angle that will get me the next field job." Emmy dug deep into her closet, heaved out her overly large Louis Vuitton suitcase—or as she liked to call it her *'I'm sorry I didn't make it to your college graduation'* gift from her mother.

She tossed out shoes as Marissa riffled through her clothes. "High heels or cowboy boots?" She threw the question over her shoulder, setting out a pair of red pumps and her barely used pair of brown cowboy boots.

"Both," Marissa answered. "Wait. Why do these cowboy boots look new? How long has it been since you used them?"

Emmy thought back to the last time she'd visited her dad's ranch. "Before college, I think. I got busy trying to make my own way in life. Those were a Christmas gift from him when my old pair started cracking from overuse."

"Wait! I got it." Marissa examined Emmy's teal and brown leather Justin's. "Do you have a pair of high-heeled cowboy ones? Those would be perfect."

"No."

"Damn. I guess you can borrow my pair. The heel is five inches tall, and the toe is pointed. And there's the cutest flower design on the side." Marissa traced a design down her leg where a boot top would be.

"Why do you even have those?" Emmy questioned.

"It's not like I'm going to go kick horse shit with them." Her friend shrugged. "I like to go to *The Urban Cowboy* and ride the bull."

Emmy lifted her eyebrow. "Ride the bull?"

Marissa's eyes twinkled with what Emmy could only call lusty mischief. "Yes, the bull. And maybe an Urban Cowboy, or two."

"You're starting to sound like Stacy."

"She's an American icon, every blossoming teen's idol. I say embrace the changing times and roll with the trends."

"I say famous parents should teach their children proper rules of society and stop with this express yourself crap." Emmy tossed out a miniskirt and a pair of jeans from her dresser and shoved them into her travel case.

"Like your mother did?"

"I thought we weren't talking about her anymore."

"Everyone in the office knows now. What do you think I was doing at my computer before we left? You can't go around being famous and expect me not to blab my mouth. Why didn't you tell me?"

"That's why. You promised you wouldn't say anything."

"I know. I'm sorry, but you shouldn't be ashamed of who you are."

"I'm trying to make it on my own, and I didn't want everyone in the office thinking I got here because of my mom."

"No one thinks that." After another scrutinizing look, Marissa let her judging squint ease, and smiled. "Anyway, I would have thought your mother taught you to be all unique and screwed up like Stacy. According to *The Click*, your mom still likes to live the fabulous life."

"The Click is a trash magazine. And my da… godfather was the one who taught me to act with grace and decorum."

"Right. You grew up on a farm with your godfather. So, cowboy life ruined you for the elite nightlife? Now, with all of your fancy etiquette and distaste for the diva life, you're only fit to catch the eye of a prince or a wall street business-man. You'll never get a party boy running around with all that uptightness." Marissa walked to the mirror and adjusted her breasts. "Cowboys don't like sophisticated women. They like party girls who aren't afraid to get down and dirty."

"Urban cowboys, maybe. And where'd you hear that?"

"From Paul." The confusion on Emmy's face must have been clear, because her friend sighed and continued, "A guy I met at *The Urban Cowboy*."

"You know there aren't any real cowboys at *The Urban Cowboy*, right? They're a bunch of executives playing country boy on the weekend, and I don't think *Paul* is using the cowboy slang of down and dirty in the right context."

"Whatever. Paul's definition is the only meaning I'll accept."

Emmy rolled her eyes. While her perky little friend was one hell of a people person, she lacked substantially in determining personal boundaries and had a soft spot for sweet talking men. A gentle whisper in her ear, and she would melt in any man's arms, or rather their beds.

Emmy stuffed a handful of her underwear in the pouch on the top of the suitcase, grabbed her hygiene items from the bathroom, and shoved them next to her underwear.

She stepped back and glared down at the luggage, sagging the middle of her bed. "If I don't come home, then I sank in a mud hole while carrying this."

"You should name your bag. That sounds like something a bimbo would do. Call him Louis."

"I'd rather call him Ralph. That's what I want to do every time my mother sends me one of these pity presents. I'd rather die before taking this thing out, but it's appropriate for my cover I guess."

"The only thing that ever died because of Louis," Marissa caressed the luggage like it was a new-born baby, "was the poor cow who gave his life to carry your undies. Don't feel too bad, though; he made one hell of a burger at *The Urban Cowboy*."

Emmy laughed. Her friend's carefree approach to life gave her a boost of energy. "Too bad I can't stuff you in Ralph and bring you with. You could help me get the scoop from Stacy."

"Speaking of Stacy." Marissa bounced on the bed and adjusted her seat. "What's she like? You were neighbors, right?"

"Sort of. She lived next to my mother, but I didn't live at home, so I've only met her a handful of times."

"At least you have an in with her."

"Now I just need to figure out an approach." Emmy mimicked Marissa's position on the bed and grabbed the pillow to hug it. How was she going to do this? She'd seen no one from that part of her life for years. Chances were Stacy wouldn't even remember who she was.

"Go in guns a blazing—in your red heels, of course. Just don't go falling for any smooth-talking cowboy and get distracted, or at least wait until after you have the story to fall for the cowboy. On second thought, don't come home without getting some country boy." Marissa rolled her eyes to the ceiling and smiled dreamily. "I'm going to live vicariously through you."

"I thought your cowboy executives were enough?"

"Why have a tofu burger when you can have angus?"

Emmy laughed at the analogy. "I'll call you every day with details."

"Atta girl." Marissa stood up from the bed with a leap.

Emmy smiled in response. Even though she had no intention of letting anyone distract her from her goal, at least she could humor her friend a little along the way. Maybe make up a fake cowboy to have a fling with and then repeat movie love scenes to her over the phone. That should keep her satisfied without having to find a man. In the meantime, Emmy needed to get her head right. It wasn't every day she had to act like a brainless twit.

"Now, what are you going to wear to the party?" Marissa rifled through the row of formal dresses pushed all the way in the back of her closet. She pulled out a red one and held it up to her chest before tossing it onto Emmy's pile of clothes to pack.

Emmy's stomach dropped. "There's going to be a party?"

Marissa chuckled. "Yep. Fancy parties and horses. High heels and cowboy boots."

*Oh, God.* She thought she was done with all of that. What in the world did she get herself into?

DUST FLEW into the open windows of the old flatbed Ford while Emmy clung to the seat as best she could. The road and surrounding hills were so familiar. She knew she'd been here before, but she couldn't put her finger on when. Most likely it was one of the many towns she'd visited with her father, or maybe even rode in a rodeo here herself. But that was long ago, and her life had been such a whirlwind between California and Montana, she never had time to make real friends... other than Stacy, that was.

The truck hit another rut and she bounced again. Of course, the cowboy behind the wheel didn't seem to mind the extra spring in the seat of the old truck as he sped down the dusty road. Emmy bounced with every bump and cringed when her elbow slammed into the door.

The cowboy next to her sat silent as the music blared—almost drowned out by the sound of the truck crushing the rocks beneath the tires.

She glanced again at him. He looked familiar, but then

11

again, she'd seen a lot of cowboys in her life. This one, though, was tall—tall, tan, and just the right kind of sexy. With arms leading into a dark blue T-shirt, bulging with muscles only years on a ranch could form.

His jaw was defined, as was that chin dimple she saw whenever he looked her way and gave a nervous smile. Why would he be nervous? It didn't matter. Marissa would have been all over this guy if they had given her the assignment.

"Goodness," Emmy yelled above the noise, hoping to sound brainless enough to seal in her facade. "My boobs are bouncing all over the place."

He ran a quick eye over the low-cut top and slowed the truck down. The noise from outside lessened and the twangy country song seemed to blare even louder out of the one speaker that still worked. The cowboy reached out and turned down the music. "Sorry about that. I'm not used to city girls riding in my truck."

"You say that like it's a bad thing." Emmy turned to sit on one hip and smooth her way-too-short, but oh so stylish, skirt. At least she'd thought to wear bicycle shorts beneath. What the heck would Stacy do in this situation? Other than jump on his lap and lick the steering wheel. "I can do anything a big ol' country boy like you can do."

"Is that so?" He sounded impressed, but not surprised.

"Yep." She flipped her gaze forward to punctuate her word, but inside her stomach dropped. If he only knew. She supposed he would find out soon enough. It was bound to get out that she grew up in Montana. "I'm Emmy Wilson."

"Emmy Wilson, huh?" His eyebrows creased and confusion flashed in his eyes for a split second. Was he expecting someone else?

"Yep. Emmy Wilson."

"The rest of the contestants are already here."

"Oh, well, I'm not a contestant. I came for the story."

"You'll have to take that up with Carl. As far as I know, you're on the roster as a contestant." He focused on the road. "I guess we'll just have to see how tough you really are in those red bale hooks you have on your feet."

"I think I can surprise you." Although she had to talk to someone about why she was there, she smiled when he glanced at her with a glimmer of something shining in his eye. She couldn't quite tell if it was appreciation mixed with challenge, or pure old calculated contempt. Either way, she would have to be careful around him.

"Like I said, you're the last one here, Ms. Wilson. All the others arrived this morning. You missed the meet and greet luncheon."

"But I got the pleasure of having you for an escort," she said dryly.

He shrugged. "I lost a bet to Big Jay."

"What was the bet?"

He stared at her for a second, as if deciding whether to tell and glanced back to the road. "I bet that Stacy Siepres would show up drunk."

"And she didn't?" Shocking, actually. The girl from her past was known for always being drunk or high.

"Big Jay bet she would make out with the first man she saw."

"And she did?"

He tipped his mouth up in a cheesy and, as her dad would say, shit eatin' grin.

She raised a single eyebrow. "So either way, you won."

His shit eatin' grin deepened, and he faced the road, turning down a long, still dusty, driveway. "Welcome to Lone Tree Hill Ranch."

"Long name." She searched the surrounding hills but couldn't see the so called lone tree.

"We just call it The Lone Tree Ranch. I guess when my

ancestors settled here there was only one tree on the hill above the ranch. I think one of them must have chopped it down cause I've never seen that tree." Jax shut the truck off and opened the door to slide out of his side of the truck. Emmy did the same, only she didn't make the landing quite as smoothly as he did. She would have, had she been wearing jeans and her boots, but she'd opted to show up looking the part of a wealthy socialite. Damn it. While she had no problem wearing a knee-length pencil skirt and button up silk blouse at work, she'd never been comfortable wearing clothes right out of a hookers closet. She had an image to uphold, though.

"Oh my God! Emmy!" a shrill scream bounced off of the rusty truck side. Emmy glanced to where Jax stood, untying the luggage—now ruined with layers of dirt and grime. She silently chuckled. Her mom would be pissed.

"I think you've got a fan here already," Jax's cowboy hat bobbed to cover what seemed to be another shit eatin' grin as Stacy bounced down the walkway from the large, white farmhouse.

"Emmy! Oh my God," Stacy repeated mindlessly as she neared. She scooped her up in a hug that squished their boobs together.

"Stacy." Thank God. She'd be able to clear this whole contestant thing up. "Jax said something about me being a contestant. I came here to get the story about the show."

"Well, yeah, but we needed another contestant last minute, so I said you'd be glad to help." She stuck her lip out in a pout. "Don't tell me you don't want to help me out. I can have someone else come do the story."

"No. No. I'll help." Her long-lost childhood friend backed away and Emmy glimpsed her makeup and fake eyelashes— only instead of the perfectly painted face she expected, Stacy hid red, swollen eyes beneath the powdery surface.

"Have you been crying?" She let the concern show on her face. Could be a story, but she was generally concerned. In all their summers together growing up, she'd never seen Stacy cry. She'd always been void of emotion. Robotic, even.

"No." Stacy sniffed, stepped away from Emmy, and flounced over to place her hand on Jax's arm as he finished yanking the last bag from the flatbed. She twisted one high-heeled, designer cowboy boot in the dirt in a move that made her butt cheek poke out from beneath her daisy dukes. Not that her top was much better. Her string bikini barely covered her nipples, let alone the rest of her boobs. Stacy pressed her chest against Jax. "I think maybe I'm allergic to the air or something."

"You mean fresh air?" Emmy murmured.

Stacy waved absentmindedly as she gazed seductively at Jax. Emmy wasn't sure why, but she wanted to either barf, curl her lip up in disgust, or rip her hair out. But she had to act like... well, like her mother. So, she let her cherry red painted lips curl in a smile. "Fresh air can do that to you. Give you allergies. I swear, it's worse than pollution sometimes."

With one last push of her perfect breasts against Jax's arm, Stacy bounced back to Emmy. "I begged them to let us be bunkmates, so Ms. McCall moved around that whore Coco Shriffer and put you where she was. I get the top." She slid a seductive look to Jax. "I'm always on top." *God, she has the attention span of a fruit fly*. Emmy flinched when she turned back to her, undeterred. "Can you believe it? When my agent called me with the idea for this gig, I was like hell yeah! A chance to be a real cowgirl? I'll take it. This will be a lot of fun."

Stacy giggled and guided Emmy toward a row of freshly whitewashed, but small, buildings. Once away from Jax's prying ears, Emmy leaned in. "Okay, why were you crying?"

Stacy shook her head. "My boyfriend just broke up with me. He was a bad influence on me, anyway," she said defensively, and then sighed, "but a lot of fun. It's heartbreaking. I don't want anyone to know, so don't put it in your article. I trust you to keep my secret Emmy." She stared at her pointedly.

"Of course."

"Good. Then let's get to our own personal bunkhouse meet and greet." Stacy lightened her step and bounced a little as she walked, causing Emmy to focus once more on trying to fit in with Stacy. Make her happy. This would be a long few weeks.

Emmy gave one last, desperate glance back to the truck, trying to find a reason to stay behind—at least for a few minutes. Long enough to get her bearings where Stacy was concerned.

To her surprise, Jax locked eyes with her and his chest rose and fell in a rhythmic chuckle. The damn jerk found humor in her misery. She glared and did what every immature, spoiled brat would do. She stuck her tongue out and then snapped her gaze forward, but not before catching the wink he sent her.

Her heart somersaulted in her chest. Holy crap, the man was sexy. The 'steal your breath, turn your insides into warm pools of jelly just because he's looking at you' kind of sexy. Maybe Marissa had the right idea. Maybe a summer fling was what she needed, but then again, she needed to remember why she was here in the first place. Playing cat and mouse with a hot cowboy would not help her get the story.

# CHAPTER 2

"*D*oes she really not remember you?" Jax McCall's neighbor and best friend, Chase, asked the question even Jax was wondering. Why didn't Emmy Wilson remember him? Was he that forgettable?

"To be fair to her, that was my blonde phase."

Chase laughed. "Oh right, you bleached your hair and listened to rock. Your dad about had a heart attack. Glad that phase didn't last."

"Everyone is entitled to one moment of confusion in life, and I definitely got over it," Jax said.

"Not long after that rodeo, if I remember correctly." His friend rested on one foot and stared off into the distance as if going through his memories.

"Yeah. Not long after," Jax repeated absently. Through the barn doors, he spotted the white bunkhouse off in the distance. Emmy was not only the goddaughter of his favorite bronc rider, but the first woman to reject him. She wasn't the last, but that didn't matter. In all honesty, he couldn't blame her for rejecting him back then. He'd been a confused teenager, green around the gills and anything but smooth.

But it was the way she went about it that was so unforgettable.

He could never forget her. From the way her lips quirked up into the cutest smile he'd ever seen on a woman, to the way she'd smelled like roses even after working her horse in the sun all day. She'd captured his attention at the rodeos his first year riding broncs, but she hadn't noticed him. Not until the night he tried to start something with her, and he got left in the dust. Literally. He hadn't forgotten about her since.

Jax didn't know why he told her about Stacy kissing him. Maybe it was the way she'd looked at him while they were bouncing down the dirt road. Like she'd finally noticed him or wanted him. Problem was, she was ten years too late. He wouldn't put himself out there for her again.

The memory of the way the breeze from her open window in his truck filled the cab with her scent caused his chest to tighten. *God.* She still smelled the same.

Jax glanced around the barn and focused on the gelding once more. "I guess she doesn't remember me. It's better that way, anyway."

"Take your keys this time. That way she can't steal your truck."

"Funny." Jax scratched his chin. "I'm not getting involved with a woman like her this time. At least I know what I'm getting with Stacy."

"Yes. Go for the emotionless robot. No strings attached, right? Couldn't have you falling in love with anyone." Chase's sister, Marni, brushed down the buckskin colt, chuckling to herself.

"Besides you, you mean?" Jax winked. Marni was more like a sister to him. There was no way he could ever fall for her—much to Chase's relief, no doubt. Still, he liked to tease her every once in a while. "Don't worry about me. I'm not ready to fall in love. Not with the ranch the way it is. I need to focus on digging us out of the dirt first."

"Do you think she knows that we know who she is? I haven't heard her tell anyone she already knows how to ride." Marni moved to another horse.

"She just got here. When did you overhear anything she's said so far?" Chase questioned.

Marni shrugged. "I was bringing some extra pillows into the bunkhouse when Stacy brought her in."

"I guess we don't know who she is. Not really." Jax moved on to the next horse they'd picked out for the High Heels to ride during the challenge. Not that it was a real challenge. More like a quick peek at what could be if the producers were to pick up the show. Still, he wanted to use his best horses. "I mean, I knew she was Tye Travers' goddaughter, but I had no idea her mother was famous."

"I think that was the point." Marni moved on to the next horse. "It sounds like they were all pretty hush-hush about her past. And she wants to keep it that way. We should probably keep this to ourselves."

"What fun is that? Plus, they are cheating bringing her in." Chase scoffed. "I'm all for calling the local press."

"Except we signed that confidentiality agreement with that tanned dude, Carl." Jax reminded. "This show isn't even guaranteed to go all the way. These are just trial episodes."

"Thank God, too." Chase tossed his brush in a nearby feeder. "We're riding in Amarillo a few days after this is done. We have to leave as soon as we can after this is over. You're driving, right?"

Jax chuckled. "I don't think we could make it to Texas in your truck."

"What about Two Socks? Did you ask your dad yet?" The hope in Chase's voice filled the barn. Poor guy. He was bound for disappointment. His father never let him ride his prized roping horse.

Jax pinched his lips tight. "Not yet. And why can't you ask him?"

"He's your dad's horse. Not mine."

"Does it have to be today?"

Chase yanked his hat off of his head and ran his hands through his hair. "I guess not. I need to know soon, though. Otherwise I need to find myself a new heeler or another horse for you."

One sorrel in the corral whinnied and trotted into a barn stall. The star on his head similar to the one Emmy's horse had back in the day.

Not that they'd gone to school together, but they'd both been on the National High School Rodeo Association circuit. Well, he'd been on it more than she had. And now he knew why. She had a different life outside of Montana and the NHSRA.

One of privilege and, if her relationship with Stacy Siepres was any sign, a lot of wild fun. So why had she rejected him all those years ago?

It wasn't that she'd rejected him that bothered him so much. It was more of the way she'd done it, and because he'd never forgotten her. Not even after she stopped doing the circuit.

He never thought he'd see her again. And definitely not like this. When he picked her up this afternoon, he hadn't expected it to be her. Yeah, the name was the same, but he'd thought he was picking up a High Heel contestant with the same name as the girl he used to know. A rich girl from New York. Not his Emmy. She'd worn a short skirt and equally tight top. Not the tight jeans and cowgirl shirt he'd seen her in at the rodeos. And it had been at least ten years later, but she was still just as beautiful.

"It's not fair that Emmy is on the High Heels team. Don't you think?" Marni ran her gaze between the men, her expression expecting someone to agree.

"Just as fair as it is to have Jax on our team."

Marni smirked. "Oh, right! I forgot he spent that summer after high school in the city."

"Me chasing a girl to the city for a few months doesn't mean I can win the High Heels contests."

"Well, it gives us a better chance than we had before." Marni tossed her brush down. "Anyway, I finished my horses," Marni announced, drawing Jax out of his thoughts.

Marni untied her horse. "Who's going to tell your dad?"

They both stared at him as he yanked the lead rope free from the knot and adjusted his hold on it. Of course it would be him. It was his dad, after all. Then again, they were practically family. "You two are wusses."

"Hey." Chase held up his hands in defense. "He's not our old man. Plus, you need to talk to him about Two Socks."

"Might as well be your home. You live here more than you do your own place." Jax ignored the second part to his friend's comment. He didn't know when he'd ask his dad to use his prized horse. The answer would be never, if he was smart.

Jax waited for Chase to untie his horse and followed his friend out of the barn to tie the mounts to the fence. On the other side of the posts, the barely broke horses his father had picked out for the Cowboy Boots to ride during the competition, kicked up dust.

"Yeah, well, your ranch needs more help than ours does." Marni popped her hip out.

"Don't let my dad hear you say that." Jax chuckled at the thought of how his dad would react. He wasn't a mean father, just brash and hardened by the rough life he'd built out in the Montana brush. He was as solid as the hundred-year-old pine trees Jax and his friends had carved their names in as kids, and just as weathered.

Chase glanced around as if looking for his dad. With one last chuckle, Jax headed for the big house. He stomped through the mudroom and straight into the kitchen where a few Network men and his father were bent over a spread of papers.

"Out you go!" His mother's stern voice made him stop dead in his tracks. She pointed the soapy spoon in her hand toward the door, splashing water on the floor. "You know better than to come into my house with horse shit on your shoes."

Jax glanced at his worn-out boots and stepped back into the mudroom. In the kitchen, the men who'd been busy seconds ago now sat staring at him, all of them standing shoeless but in various shades of socks.

His father just shook his head and chuckled as Jax's mother went back to doing the dishes.

The men bent over the papers again. "The goal here is to make Stacy look like a small town sweetheart. We're talking as morally conscious as a preacher's daughter."

Jax mentally laughed. He couldn't wait to see how they pulled that one off. The woman in question was anything but morally conscious. He might enjoy a good kiss with her now and then, but he wasn't dumb enough to do anything more than that with her.

"Sorry, Mama." He slipped off his boots, and once again entered the kitchen. "Pop. The horses are ready for the first challenge."

"Great." His father didn't bother to look up from whatever he was reading.

"And Ms. Wilson is settled in?" Carl, the man with the bad, fake tan asked. "She's the key to this whole operation."

"Stacy is showing her the bunkhouse now." Confused at

why Emmy was important, but not having the time to question Carl further, Jax turned to his father. "Got a second, Pop?"

His dad scowled but nodded. He sent the three men a stare that left little to question.

"I just put some fresh coffee and cookies out on the front porch, and I'm brewing more so go make room for it." His mother shooed the men away. Jax didn't miss the irritated frown on Carl's face. He tried not to smile. If the man thought he was really in charge of this whole brouhaha, he'd made a mistake setting it up at his parent's ranch. Here, his father ran the show, and his mother ran his father.

Jax waited until the men left before turning to his dad. "I know this isn't the right time to ask, but there's a rodeo in Amarillo a few days after this thing ends. I was hoping I could use Two Socks."

"I thought you were a bronc rider," his dad growled out. "You don't need my horse for that."

"Chase needs a heeler. I'll owe you."

"Absolutely not. I'm already elbow deep in the last favor you asked me." His dad waved toward where the three men had disappeared and stood to pour himself a cup of coffee from the fresh pot brewing.

"I was trying to help you save the ranch." Jax let his irritation out with his words. The damned man was impossible. "They gave us enough money to keep us afloat until—"

"Until what? You win the finals?" His dad scoffed.

"No. Until you come up with a better plan."

His father scraped his chair across the floor as he straightened it out and sat. "You're not using Two Socks. Take the mare you're training."

"She isn't ready."

"Then I guess you don't team rope. Chase will have to find another heeler." His father picked up one of the papers he'd been examining. "Now, tell those city guys to come back in here, and then wrangle the contestants."

Jax tapped his fist on the tabletop before yanking his shoes back on in the mudroom. That talk had gone just about how he'd thought it would. His only regret was that he would disappoint yet another person when he told Chase he couldn't use Two Socks.

He seemed to do that a lot lately.

"Okay, listen up," Stacy clapped her hands to get the attention of the two other girls in the bunkhouse. "This is our last moment without the cameras in our face every minute of the day, so let's make it count. But remember, this is between us only. So, we're going to fill out this confidentiality contract that I had my lawyer draw up. I've already sent it to most of your lawyers as well. They should have already talked to you."

Stacy passed out the paper and Emmy ran a quick eye over it as the others signed it. She'd definitely not gotten this paper before. Not that it was a bad thing. The way they worded this, it may just save her mother's secret from leaking out if both of Emmy's worlds somehow collided here at The Lone Tree Ranch. "Why the secrecy, Stacy?"

"To protect us, duh." She turned back to the group. "Everyone, this is my neighbor, Emmy. She's Rochelle Wilson's daughter."

The other two girls murmured their approval and made her stomach sink. She was not the sort to be comfortable around people who liked her for who her mother was. She was the sort who valued true friendship and honest relationships.

Ever since she was younger, she couldn't stand shallow

people. She'd done her best to avoid them. No matter how she had to do it. Like when she'd visited her mother and lied to Stacy about not being home when she really just hid in her house doing her schoolwork. Since she'd been homeschooled and tutored, she always had an excuse when needed.

Or when she'd left that cowboy to find his way down the mountain after she'd let herself be talked into attending one of the bonfire parties after her last rodeo. Ever since then she'd given up the competitive life and focused instead on her studies. Now here she was, a journalist undercover as a competitor in a contest that mirrored both of her lives.

Fate was ironic that way.

Stacy continued, interrupting Emmy's thoughts, "We have our first challenge today, so we need to be tough. T-O-U-F, tough."

*God, was she really this dense?* Doubtful. When they were kids, Stacy had been a straight-A student, not at all the brainless twit she pretended to be now. Chances were, it was all an act, a show to further her career. "I think you mean G-H."

"Oh, yeah, thanks Emmy. Emmy's smart. She went to college and everything." Stacy turned to face her. "When there's a challenge where we need someone smart, you're it, girl."

"Thanks," Emmy drawled. Somehow, she didn't think the folks who masterminded this show would care about smarts. Most likely they were banking on Stacy spouting off a few more of her brainless, but Emmy suspected, well thought out comments.

Stacy clapped again. "Like I was saying, we need to be T-O-G-H, tough. Now, I'd like to have a little get to know you session within our group." She glanced at her ten-thousand dollar watch. "The challenge doesn't start for another half of an hour, so let's all sit. I don't like to say Indian style, because it's offensive, so let's all sit Native American style."

Stacy folded one leg under the other in a show of grace, followed closely by the other two women in the bunkhouse. Emmy glanced around at the three porcelain faces that watched her until she too dropped to sit cross-legged on the ground.

Emmy adjusted her seat and studied the group, stopping at Stacy—her shorts just a little too revealing. She turned her head, but Emmy covered the vision of Stacy's exposed crotch with her hand, anyway. "Your shorts are a little short. Could you please put on some panties?"

Stacy giggled and adjusted her daisy dukes. "I have panties on, silly. I found this new style of G-string. It's made by Larenzo on Rodeo Drive." She ran a quick eye over the other two girls. "Speaking of Rodeo, did you know that they don't even say the word right over here? In their native tongue it's pronounced rodeo, like road-e-o."

"In their native tongue?" Emmy tried not to let her voice sound too... judgey. "They aren't from another country. A rodeo is an event, not a place."

"Ah. I know, silly." Stacy giggled and reached behind her to pull out a joint. "Anyhow, let's get to the game. What we do here is take a hit and then say something about ourselves. If anyone else has ever experienced the same thing, then kiss the person holding the roach. Tongue is unnecessary but is encouraged. Second base is also permitted while kissing."

*What the hell?* Emmy's heart pounded. Never in her life had she kissed another girl, and she didn't want to start now. She mentally rolled her eyes. What shit journalists had to do for a story. "Shouldn't there be, oh I don't know, men here for this game?"

Stacy shrugged. "Usually, but I want to get close to you girls, and this is my favorite ice breaker game. I'll start."

She lit the joint and took a deep inhale, held it, and then slowly let it out. "I've made love to a girl before."

*Okay. This could be an information gold mine.* Mental note, Stacy has made love to a girl. Thankfully, Emmy had not.

One girl sat up on her knees and Stacy kissed her.

Emmy swallowed the vomit burning the back of her throat as it threatened to come up. She studied her watch, not that she knew what time the events started, but it was the only thing she could do that didn't force her to watch the spectacle before her.

*Oh, my God. Thirty seconds?* The slurping sound filled the room until finally they separated. Stacy passed the joint to Julie—the one woman who hadn't yet earned a place in whoreville in Emmy's book.

Emmy's heart pounded in her chest as Julie told her truth. Please, Lord. Don't let her say anything that Emmy had done. She could always lie. No one knew about her past few years except those few acquaintances from college. And none of them were here. A wave of relief spread through Emmy. Maybe she could get through this without having to play the dumb game.

Her moment of reprise was short lived when Julie passed the joint to her. What was she going to do now? Emmy was straight laced. She had never kissed a girl before and definitely done nothing else with one. Hell, she barely drank alcohol, let alone did drugs.

The women stared at her, waiting. She had to do something. She pretended to take a hit, hoping they wouldn't see too clearly through the smoke in the room. Now what truth could she tell that no one else would have done? "I went to New York University."

Stacy laughed. "No, something new. We already know you went to college."

*Shit. What now? Hurry, think of something.* She scrambled through her memories for something. Anything. "I have been arrested."

27

Damn it! *Dumb choice, Emmy.*

"Really? You?" Stacy stared at her in disbelief, but then stood on her knees along with the other girl—who Emmy was starting to believe was lying about her sordid past to get Stacy to like her. Either that or the two of them were an awful lot alike.

"Uh," she mumbled, and searched the ground around her for something to use as an excuse. Nothing jumped out, except maybe her heart as it sped up the closer Stacy got.

"Don't be scared," Stacy crooned. "I'm a really good kisser, and what happens here stays here. Secrets, Emmy."

"I… I'm not scared, per se." More like grossed out, not interested… okay, a bit scared. "I—"

A loud knock echoed through the room, and relief flowed through Emmy. She jumped to her feet, eating the distance to the door and taking a deep breath. She didn't want to make out with any of the women in the room, but she sure as hell wanted to kiss whoever had knocked.

"Time for the first challenge," Jax's voice boomed from outside. Of course it would be him. Either way, she was grateful. Emmy yanked the door open and tried not to let him see her relief.

"What's going on here?" Jax grinned and propped his hand on the doorjamb while the two other people standing behind him craned their necks to look inside.

Like any good girl caught doing something bad, Emmy hid the drug behind her back.

"We were just about to come out." Emmy glanced back, hoping the other women would back her up. Instead, Stacy grabbed the joint from her fingers, puffed, and passed it along.

"I see that." Jax laughed. "Not enjoying yourself, Ms. Wilson?"

He sounded a little too happy about her situation. Emmy tried not to frown.

"I'm not much of a party game person." What else could she say that would keep her identity intact but make an excuse for not joining in on the High Heel's fun? She scratched her head. "Uh. We were getting to know each other. I guess."

"It's not like weed is illegal here, Emmy. Plus, I found out we're a lot alike," Stacy crooned. Emmy turned as Stacy smoothed Coco's hair and stared at her like she was falling in love.

"I'm sure we did that earlier at the luncheon." Jax hooked his thumbs through his belt loops. "But I'd love to get to know you girls a little better. Let me know next time and I'll join you."

Emmy rolled her eyes, but Stacy giggled and stood.

"Of course you can join." Stacy pushed past Emmy and, once again, stuck her tongue down Mr. Perfect Cowboy's face.

The woman had no boundaries—not that that was a story. These days no one had boundaries.

Emmy cleared her throat and slipped past the love birds, stopping briefly to see the odd look on the man and woman who stood behind Jax. Staring. At her. Recognition shone from their eyes. She forced a smile, hoping that they recognized her as the Beverly Hill's socialite and not as Tye Traver's goddaughter. It might look like she was here to cheat. Had they been to one of the rodeos she'd attended? It wasn't like she was on the circuit long. Just one season. Hopefully, no one would recognize her. "I… I'm ready for the challenge."

Jax lifted his head from Stacy with a suction sound and turned to give Emmy a once over. "You may want to change. Maybe put on some boots."

"I'm in boots, silly," Stacy used her palm to bring his face to look back at her.

He glanced down, whether to stare at Stacy's exposed boobs or boots, Emmy wasn't sure. Either way, breasts were stuck in his face. Not that Emmy was jealous. She didn't need a man like Jax ruining this story for her.

Damn. The story. She'd been so frantic to find a way out of the bunkhouse she'd forgotten to ask questions. Prod Stacy for nibbles of information.

Julie and Coco bustled past her with assurances to the Cowboy Boots that they had no intention of changing their heels.

She glanced down to her bright red pumps, now making her want to rip off her foot from the pain searing up her calves. Damn. She should have taken Marissa up on the offer to borrow her fancy heeled boots. She knew she'd regret her next statement, but had to do it for the cover. "I'll keep my heels on too."

The two other cowboys smirked while Jax gave a one-shouldered shrug and waved toward the barn. "Suit yourself. The other contestants are waiting."

In a few minutes, a crowd of people came into view, and gathered around the entrance to a barn. Emmy's stomach fluttered, and her heart kicked up in speed. This was real. Her face would be plastered all over reality television, and she had to act like the dimwit she tried hard not to be.

An announcer's voice boomed from somewhere in the crowd, directing them to the front of the barn. Shit! Why hadn't Viv given her an earlier flight? She had no idea who anyone was. But at least she knew who was on her team.

"Welcome, welcome contestants." The handsome television host, Carl Rogers, looked to Emmy. "Ms. Wilson. Good to meet you. Finally."

Her heart jumped to her throat at being in the spotlight

so unexpectedly, but she smiled and nodded sweetly. "Good to be here, Carl."

The host concentrated once more on the crowd and contestants and waved toward the open barn door. "Welcome to the first challenge."

Emmy peeked around the announcer at the row of horses. On the fence post next to each mount sat saddles. Whatever the contest was, it involved horses. Horses she could do. Although in heels it would be rough.

"All right contestants. For the preview we've put together three competitions: one that favors the Cowboy Boots, one that's neutral, and one that favors the High Heels. Today is the first Cowboy Boot competition. You will saddle your horse and ride it through the arena," Carl continued. "Ride to the other side where you will dismount, take the rope off the saddle, stand behind the line, and rope the dummy steer. The first person to make it to the finish line wins for their team. All team members must complete the challenge. To make it fair, Cowboy Boots, you will first have to catch your horses in the corral, and I must warn you, they are a feisty bunch." Carl pointed to a large pen with six horses stomping and churning up dust, their heads thrown high and whinnies coming from deep within the small herd. "High Heels, pay close attention to Mr. McCall as he shows you how to saddle a horse."

An older man made his way next to Carl and began the demonstration. He was shorter than Jax, but had the same chiseled features, although the older McCall wore them with a weathered definition that spoke of hard days in the saddle.

Once he finished, Carl called for the contestants to take their places, so Emmy stumbled through the powdery dirt in her six-inch heels and took her position next to a pretty little brown mare. She studied the saddle slung over the fence and mentally calculated her moves for the contest. Time crawled by without another word from the announcer. Emmy turned to find out what the holdup was. Twenty feet away, Stacy stood in the midst of a massive makeover. People gathered around her, swiping makeup over her face and tugging ferociously at her body.

Emmy glanced down at her own outfit. *Shit!* Why the hell had she chosen to wear the damned skirt? Too bad she didn't have an entourage to give her a wardrobe change. Not that she'd enjoy the fuss. At the very least, she should have thought to change after getting to the ranch.

Once Stacy emerged looking like a modern day, trouser wearing Laura Ingalls, the announcer waved to the crew and people fussed around the cameras. Emmy took a quick glance around to the rest of the High Heel contestants, all confused and staring blankly at the saddles.

"Contestants, take your positions," Carl called as Stacy broke free of her entourage.

Inside the second corral, the Cowboy Boots gathered around the gate to the back pen while outside the High Heels took their spots next to the horses. Emmy's chest twisted in anticipation. It had been years since she'd ridden a horse, but she could still remember the exhilaration of being on the back of one as it raced down the corral with the wind rushing past her ears. And the way her stomach flipped with each beat of her horse's hooves. She'd lean into the turn, not really needing to rein her well-trained horse. He knew what to do and loved every minute of the run. Truth was, she couldn't wait to swing her leg over the saddle again.

Her days in the arena were the only ones she'd ever truly enjoyed.

"Action," a man from the crowd called and Carl blew the whistle, drawing Emmy from her thoughts.

She jumped toward the fence, only to wrench her foot sideways as her heels hit a divot in the ground. She fell forward and grabbed onto the pommel of the saddle. Except it wasn't tied to anything, so instead of righting herself, she fell in a heap of leather and short skirts.

"Should have worn better shoes." Jax's voice filled the space around her. "I tried to warn you."

Emmy's heart fluttered as Jax stepped up next to her and tied his horse to the post. She should come up with some smart ass reply but laying in the dirt the way she was with her skirt barely covering her ass, she would just make him laugh.

"I'm thinking you were right, but don't worry about me." She reached down, unbuckled the strap, and yanked her shoes off, tossing them under the fence as though they hadn't cost her almost a thousand dollars.

It took a second to stand upright and scoop up both the saddle and blanket. Memories of days with her horse, Butterscotch, swirled through her mind as she swung the blanket and saddle up together over the horse's back. The mare sidled to the left—the possibility of the horse stepping straight onto her bare feet at the forefront of her mind. God, that would hurt.

But she didn't care. She never did. Then again, she'd been young and dumb back then.

Emmy yanked the cinch tighter, checked to ensure it was secure, and slipped the bridle over the horse's head. On an impulse, she blew a kiss to Jax, and then swung into the saddle without a care to the way her skirt flew up. Her legs chaffed where her shorts met the hard leather, but she didn't care. It's not like she was riding more than a few yards.

She turned to ride out of the barn when her team caught her attention. The women had yet to toss the blanket over the horse's back. The polite thing to do would be to help them out. Show them how to do it. Then again, isn't that what Jax's father had done a few minutes ago?

Next to her, Jax slapped the stirrup down after checking the cinch. No time. If she wanted to win, she'd have to go now. She'd come back for them if they still needed help.

"Use your whole body to heave it onto the horses," she yelled. "Tie the leather strap like a man's tie." When no one responded, she gave up and rode toward the arena.

She eased the latch on the gate open and maneuvered the mare through. Once the horse cleared the opening, she kicked her bare feet against her horse's side to urge her to run. In a few breaths, she reached the hay bale steer heads and leapt from the saddle to land in the hot powdery dirt. She grabbed her rope and tried not to think about the burn from the sand beneath her toes when thundering hoof beats reached her ears. She turned in time to see Jax struggle with his wild mount. She'd better hurry. Years of practice with her dad flowed through her loop when Emmy pivoted and, in less than a heartbeat, roped the steer's head. She yanked the lasso taut as another rope soared over her head to drop over the head on the bale beside hers.

She turned a smug smile to Jax as cheers rose from the crowd on the other side of the fence. "Beat ya to it."

"What the hell was that?" He walked toward the steer heads, loosened his rope, and wound them into a loop. "Is there something you want to tell me, Bobcat? A secret you're just dying to tell? Like that you've done this before?" He nodded toward the hay. "One might even say you were a professional."

"I've never competed in roping before." Well, it wasn't a lie. She'd barrel raced as a teen. That didn't mean her dad hadn't taught her a thing or two. "And Bobcat, really?"

Emmy swiped the sweat from her brow, hoping to change the subject. Still, her heart raced at Jax's comment, and the name sounded so familiar. One she'd heard before when she was younger. That couldn't be. The blonde cowboy who'd called her that was so different from the man before her now. Her heart pounded against her rib cage. Did Jax know about her past?

I mean, Viv had mostly figured out who she was fairly easily, despite her and her mother's efforts to keep her past a secret. It's possible they already knew who her father was. What would her mom do then? Have a stroke, most likely.

She hated Emmy's dad.

Jax loosened his rope from around the spearhead and wound it up, nodding toward her bare, sand burnt feet. "I figure you're crazier than a bobcat caught in a snare trap."

"Yes, but I beat you." Relieved he didn't press her with more questions, she shrugged and threw another grin as the Cowboy Boots and one of the High Heel contestants clamored through the gate.

"Is that how it's going to be?" His light blue eyes turned darker and his mouth curved into a smile she'd only seen on a cartoon wolf. It was sexy. Really sexy.

She kinda enjoyed making him smile like that. It meant he was at least a little intrigued by her. Maybe she could let herself experience a summer fling with a cowboy. Emmy tried not to chuckle out loud. Now that was something she'd never done. Almost, but not quite. "I suppose it is."

He lowered his eyelids and tipped his head down until his hat shrouded them in secrecy. Her breath hitched when he stared into her eyes. His reflected deep pools of judgement, but not in a bad way. In a way that made her insides flutter.

The pulse in her wrists thumped as he stood trying to read her. The damned man gave a slow once over of her body as if imagining how she would look naked. No doubt trying to make her nerves bunch, but she couldn't let him get into her head. She held his stare.

After a while, he returned his wolfish smile, lifted one

eyebrow, and turned to toss his rope over his pommel. "I like a challenge."

She struggled to catch the breath he'd stolen while shrouding them in secrecy and stepped back, needing distance to help gain control of her riotous insides.

Stacy yelped as she rode out of the barn, drawing Emmy's attention. The woman bobbed, belly down over the tilting saddle as her horse followed behind Coco's gelding. Coco lead her horse through the gate, apparently opting not to even attempt to ride.

"I broke one of my nails," Stacy shouted as her hair slipped off her shoulder with each bounce of the horse's gate. It shielded her face, blocking her eyes. Emmy assumed she was talking to her, but in all honesty, she didn't know. Chances were, Stacy just shouted, hoping to catch at least one sympathetic ear.

Emmy turned to Jax, whispering, "You must not like too much of a challenge. Stacy is as easy as they come."

Jax mounted his horse while his team roped their steer heads with ease. "Jealous?"

*A little.* "Nope. This may come as a shocker to you, cowboy, but not all women want to fall right into your lap just cause you smile at them."

"I'm always up for a challenge." He winked and sent her heart into a flutter.

She shook her head to rid herself of the haze he'd caused. The damned man was cockier than a rooster in a henhouse.

"Emmy, did you win?" Stacy's voice bounced with every step of her horse as she neared. "Oh, Jax. Help me down."

Emmy stared at the girl's butt stuck in the air while her head bobbed near the horse's side. Stacy yelped again when Jax eased her from the saddle. She grabbed her lasso, tilted her head to the side, and scratched her scalp. "How do you work this thing, Emmy?"

Emmy did a quick survey of her team as they struggled to get the rope around the steer's head. She turned back to Jax and motioned toward her team. "If you'll excuse me."

He extended his arm the same way she did as his team coiled their ropes and walked toward their horses. "The arena is all yours."

"Thanks." Emmy turned to her team of dimwits and put on her ditzy persona once more as she gave them a roping lesson. She needed to take care from now on to keep her cover up, especially in front of Stacy and the cameras. Except Jax watched her like he could see into her soul and had discovered her secret.

# CHAPTER 3

*J*ax waited for the crowd to dissipate, all the while watching Emmy teach her team the basics of throwing a loop. God, she was just as beautiful and spunky as ever. The perfect woman. Perfectly wrong for him.

"I thought you weren't going to fall for Emmy again." Marni lead her horse to stand next to his.

"I'm not."

"You sure did a lot of flirting for a man who's not trying to get the girl."

Jax threw her a sideways glance. "Don't you have a job to do?"

Across the arena, Emmy turned away from her group and headed into the barn with her horse. The others, however, let go of their mounts and filtered out of the arena.

Marni sighed. "I guess I'll go collect the horses."

The crew went about their business. With one quick look around to make sure no one else saw, Jax followed Emmy inside. If he'd had any doubt before about who she was, he certainly didn't now. Not with the way she'd yanked those ankle bending heels off and roped the steer's head.

The question was, did she remember him? If she did, she gave no indication of it. He couldn't blame her. It was dark the first time he'd ever gotten the guts to talk to her after watching her all year at the various rodeos. He'd been a coward back then.

Not now. By the time he made his way past the crowd of people and into the barn, Emmy had slung the saddle off the horse and settled it onto a nearby bale of hay. She glanced up at him. "Hey."

"Hey yourself." He tied his horse up in front of a stall and unsaddled him. Soon his friends would find their way inside with the rest of the horses. If he wanted to talk to her in private—see if she remembered him even a little—now was his chance.

Except he couldn't seem to find the words he needed. What did she do to him? Ever since she'd turned him down, he'd been a ladies' man, keeping himself at a distance emotionally, not wanting to get hurt again. *Damn her.*

The silence grew between them as he watched her work out of the corner of his eyes. The way her hips swayed with each step as she went about brushing the horse down caused instant heat to flood his chest. Memories of the way she'd looked in the firelight that night filtered through his mind. He'd thought she was pretty back then. Back when he'd also believed he was grown enough to fall in love with only a smile from a pretty girl like Emmy.

Now she was downright stunning, and the same thoughts flirted with his heart.

He couldn't let himself fall in love with her again, but that didn't mean he couldn't push his limits. Maybe he should test her, and see if she remembered him the way he did her.

Still barefoot, Emmy stepped gingerly around a pile of

horse shit, which made him smile. She was still as brazen and carefree as she was that night on the mountainside. And still just as barefoot. He wasn't lying when he called her crazy. Doing anything with horses barefoot was downright insane, but she somehow made it adorable.

On a quick thought, Jax ducked inside the tack room and grabbed the muck boots his mother kept stored in the corner. He brushed off the crusted over mud. "Here. These might help."

Her green eyes sparkled with something that stole his breath, and all he could think about was how soft the skin on the side of her face would feel if he ran his calloused hands down her cheek and neck, and how right it would feel to have her press against him, begging to be held.

He needed to get ahold of himself. He came in here to see if she even remembered him. That was it. He didn't want another chance with Emmy Wilson.

"What was that back there?" He thumbed in the arena's direction, hoping to open the conversation up.

Her lashes fluttered down. She snapped her head away from him, avoiding his gaze. "Who said a High Heel couldn't know how to ride a horse?"

"And rope?"

Emmy blinked a few times and searched the rafters. He assumed it was to find the answers. After a few seconds, she pierced him with a determined stare and extended her hands out. "You caught me. I learned how to rope when I was younger."

Honesty. At least a little. She'd given him that much. He leaned against the fence, hoping his pose showed a calm he didn't feel. What he wanted were answers to questions he hadn't asked yet. How was he going to even broach the topic? "Is there something we should know about you, Bobcat?"

"Why, cowboy? I thought you wanted to get to know Stacy." She took the boots and yanked them onto her feet.

He concentrated on flipping the stirrup over the pommel of his saddle and yanking at the cinch. Was that a touch of jealousy?

God! He had to stop being such a wuss! He was Jax McCall, for hell's sake. He wasn't as famous as Emmy's godfather, but he was a damned good bronc rider and had won a few rodeos in his day. Why the hell did he turn so damned weak every time she looked at him?

"Stacy is a bit too wild for my taste. I prefer someone who isn't afraid to ride a horse barefoot or go mudding up in the hills at night." Like they'd done during the party at Snowy Pond Meadow, right before they started the bonfire. But that part, he left out.

Her eyebrows creased in the middle ever so slightly. Did she remember?

"What's mudding?" Her voice changed and took on a light, confused tone. He couldn't tell if it was fake or not. There were definitely two different Emmy's, but he preferred the one that had bantered with him after roping the steer head.

"I think there's more to you than you're letting people see."

She giggled and adjusted her shirt. "Oh, I don't know. There's not much more to me than what you've seen."

"I disagree." He'd be a moron if he didn't follow the movements of her hands as she so clearly drew attention to her breasts. God, they were perfect, just like the rest of her. His body hardened in response. If she was trying to draw his attention away from the conversation, it was working. *Damn it.*

Fine. She wanted to play this game. He would, too. He took a step closer to her, towering over her until she tilted her head back to peer up at him. Her mouth was so close all he had to do was move a few inches, and he'd be able to taste her again. The scent of her stirred his already tightened core even more. It took everything he possessed not to give in, lift her in the air, and take her to the spot in the barn's corner where he liked to sneak naps.

"You're playing a dangerous game, Ms. Wilson," he warned. "I don't think you know what you're doing."

"Oh. I think I do." She squared her shoulders toward him and walked her fingers up the buttons on his shirt. His breath caught the second she touched him. The only thing stopping him from scooping her into his arms and making love to her was the gentle pressure from her fingertips grounding him to the moment.

He caught her wrist when she made it to his top button. "You have no idea who I am. Do you?"

"Should I? Are you famous or something? At an event like this, that wouldn't surprise me."

He let her wrist go and stepped back. Needing to distance himself from the heat of her body. Did she truly not know who he was, or was she hiding that the way she was hiding who her godfather was? "Nope. I'm just a Cowboy Boot. My question is, are you just a High Heel?"

She shrugged, and her demeanor changed as she moved to put her horse in the stall. "Is anyone really just one thing?"

"That's a little deep for the Emmy who played the get to know you game with Stacy earlier today."

"Are we done here?" She closed the gate and plopped her hands on her hips.

Jax took a step sideways to open up a path past him. The air around him heated when she brushed past. Her scent filling his senses once more. His body responded again. What he wanted to do was tug her back to him and kiss her, make her remember that night, and show her she was wrong for walking away from him.

Instead, he let her go.

By the time Emmy disappeared into the fading daylight outside the barn, Chase was walking through leading two horses. Thank God he hadn't showed up earlier.

"She is definitely Tye Travers' goddaughter." Jax heaved Emmy's saddle up from the hay bale and tossed it onto a sawhorse in the tack room. He returned to his horse to brush her down. "Did you see how she took her shoes off?"

"So, because she took her shoes off that means she's Tye's goddaughter?"

"Yep." Jax wiped the sweat off his forehead and then shoved his cowboy hat back down on his head.

"I don't understand."

"You probably wouldn't. You left the party early."

"Which night was it again?" Chase looked at him like he'd grown a second head.

"That night after the rodeo in town when we all went up to the lake, and she left me on the mountain. You picked me up halfway down the road."

"Ah. Right. We found your truck at the fairgrounds, keys in the ignition. What about it?"

"She went the whole night without shoes."

"And?"

"She was riding her horse with that rodeo queen you hooked up with that night. Only Emmy didn't have shoes on then either. When the girls got into my truck to go up to the party, all Emmy had on were flip-flops."

"So?"

"On a mountain in Montana. Where we sometimes get snow in August."

"And this is the same girl who stole your truck and made

you walk down the mountain alone? Did she take your boots too?"

"Funny." Jax corralled his horse and went to help Chase with the other mounts. "It wouldn't have happened if you didn't take off with the rodeo queen and leave us alone up there. I mean, hell, Emmy had barely even noticed I existed. I was just a ride to her. You were the one that had invited her and the rodeo queen to party with us at Snowy Pond Meadow."

Chase shrugged. "You'd have left too if you got with Ms. Broadwater County that night. What exactly did you do to make Emmy leave you on the mountain, anyway?"

Jax frowned. The last thing he wanted was for his friend to find out just what sort of idiot he'd been back then. Plus, he honestly had no idea what he'd done. She'd just left. "I don't want to talk about it. Can you just keep Stacy occupied?"

"You want Stacy to fall on my sword instead of yours? Fine. But you will have to face Emmy sometime. The question is, are you going to walk away or fall for her all over again?"

## CHAPTER 4

"*No* cameras today?" Emmy twisted the pen in her fingers as she sat on the stool at the counter, waiting for Stacy to respond. It had been several days of waiting and hanging out. For what she wasn't sure, but whatever it was they were all in limbo.

She'd barely seen Jax since that moment in the barn. Honestly, she got the feeling that he'd been avoiding her. So, she kept busy following the High Heels through their morning yoga, massive wardrobe issues, and afternoon tokes. Chase and Marni had taken to giving the High Heels lessons on how to ride, and Emmy went along, needing to feel the freedom riding horses gave her.

Today, though, was different. Today, Stacy had gone all business and then called her in for a private meeting.

"I sent them away so I could talk to you. They'll be back soon, though, so we should get on it."

"So, what is this whole thing about, anyway?" If Emmy hadn't just seen her neighbor changing out of her mini skirt a mere second ago, she'd swear Stacy belonged in a country kitchen.

With a frilly apron protecting a long demure dress, and her hair in a low ponytail slung loosely over her shoulder, one would almost think she was a different person than the Stacy Siepres who'd made out with more than one person just a few days ago.

Stacy dipped a wooden spoon into a bowl and stirred. This change of appearance piqued Emmy's interest, for sure. What was the goal of this whole thing? "I've never seen you wear a dress that long. Not even when you were a kid."

Stacy stopped what she was doing and peeked down the hallway across the kitchen from where she stood. "Okay, but you can't tell anyone. You signed an agreement. And I'm only telling you because we have secrets, you and I. Plus, you're going to help me with your article about my show."

"Okay," Emmy said slowly.

"It's a preview for my upcoming reality show proposal. I've been waiting for more funding from my dad, but he's been busy. In the meantime, Carl and I were ironing out some legal stuff with Coco's lawyer. But I got another investor instead so we can move on today."

"Your show. High Heels and Cowboy Boots?" Emmy jotted down a note in the small notebook she'd brought with.

"Yes. I need this to be a success, and I need your help to do it."

"So, you brought me in to help you show the world that you've changed? Why me specifically?"

Stacy stirred whatever concoction she was mixing up. "Your mom told me you'd graduated from college and needed a good gig to get your career up and going. Plus, she gave me the idea for the confidentiality thing. I knew I could trust you to keep quiet and write what I want you to write."

*Damn it, Mom!* Emmy struggled not to show Stacy just how pissed she was at her words. Not that she was ungrateful, but she'd honestly thought she'd get this far on her own and not because of her mom. That's what she'd wanted, anyway. Her mom always interfered. "What exactly are you expecting from this article?"

Stacy flipped her spoon through the air, flipping chocolate goo across the counter. "Make me look like I'm an entirely different person. Like I'm totally country and like a prude. I'll have the crew give you some pictures of me doing things like baking." She held up the bowl. "And riding horses and stuff. We've been taking those promos shots while we waited. But I need to look like I belong here."

"All to promote a show?" Emmy scrunched her face. Why would Stacy need to convince the world she was a changed woman to sell a show she's producing? It wasn't like people looked down on that stuff anymore. Hell, she'd probably make the show more successful with a few wild moments in the press.

"I mean, yeah to sell the show, but also because I need people to think I've changed. I need my dad to think I've changed."

"But you haven't," she stated.

"Are you going to help me or not?" Stacy popped a hip out and glared. "I can easily get another reporter. I was just doing your mother a favor."

As much as she wanted to toss the job in her mother's face and walk away, doing so would be career suicide. But how exactly was she going to fix Stacy's reputation with one article? "No. I'll help."

"Great." Stacy dropped the bowl on the table, grabbed a square brownie pan, and poured the batter inside. "So, what I want is you to talk about how I'm doing all this homemaker stuff. Just immersing myself in country life. Make it known that I can handle being a farmer's wife."

Emmy tugged at her earlobe. "Um… what?"

"I want you to paint the picture I am the perfect farmer's

47

wife. Like that baker lady with the cooking show. I love her cookbook!" Stacy squinted. "That's what people like of hers, right? I mean, I haven't used it myself. I don't cook, but I love the cover. I'm not actually as good as her, but I need people to think it. Also, is there any way to get this article in a cowboy magazine?"

"Why magazines?"

"So the ranchers and stuff will see my show and watch it. Duh."

"Um… Okay. I'll look into it. They may not have time to stop working their ranch just to watch the show, but I'll try." Emmy jotted that down in her notebook, still confused at why Stacy was going all in for this ruse. It was almost as if she had someone specific she was trying to impress. Either way, Emmy would do the article. Not that she thought it would help the way Stacy believed.

"So, you made brownies? Where d'you learn to do that?"

Stacy slid the pan into the pre-heated oven. "Oh, I've known how to make these for a while now. It's my special recipe, and I only use the best pot. Want one when they're done?"

"No, thanks."

Stacy shrugged and sat on a stool next to Emmy. "Suit yourself. We're about to do another challenge, and its way more fun this way."

"How are you doing all of this? It's your show, right?"

"Well, actually my dad is producing it. He wants some preview episodes before he commits, so he let me take a small crew and hire a few people to come on. If he likes it, then we'll do the whole season. He put me in charge as the producer here, but I'm more of like partners with Carl. He's doing all the legwork, and I'm just doing the ideas and like starring in it. It's a win for us both. Carl needed to get his career back on track. And I need the good girl exposure. I mean, I might come up with a good storyline or something, and we'll just go with it."

"What about this other investor?"

"Oh, that?" Stacy waved off her comment. "That's just me wanting to give you guys something back. My dad wasn't going for it so a friend of mine is investing, but she wants to keep it a secret. For now. This next challenge we're going to give away a prize to the winners."

"So is a hot relationship with a cowboy part of your plan?"

"Jealous?" Stacy chuckled. "That's just normal off-camera fun. Why? Do you want a chance at Jax? Just let me know and he's all yours. I was only trying to get over my ex, anyway."

"No, I... I was just getting the facts for my story."

"Right." Stacy rolled her eyes. "You know, in all the years we knew each other I only saw you date like three guys."

She didn't tell her about the few boyfriends she'd had during college. As far as Stacy knew, Emmy's life only happened in California. "I have to really like a guy before I give my heart to him."

"Give your heart to him?" Stacy snickered. "We're talking about sex here, Emmy. Not falling in love. You need to let loose a little." Stacy shook Emmy's shoulders as if she were shaking the prude out of her.

"So I need to let loose, and you need to tighten up. I guess we make a good pair here."

"Right! Good point," Stacy stopped shaking her. "So we're making sure everything on this show makes me look good. I need to make sure people see me single, independent, and loving the country life. I might even buy a little farm after this. If he sees the show, and it works out the way I want."

"He? Your dad?"

Stacy snapped her gaze to Emmy and her eyes widened for a split second. "Sure. My dad. My fans. Who knows, maybe one of these hot, rich ranchers will scoop me up and let me ride his horse."

"Rich rancher," Emmy repeated. Well, no matter what happened with the show, Emmy hoped Stacy could figure life out. Meet a nice man who would tame her a little. Hell, maybe even a cowboy.

The oven beeped. Stacy hopped from her perch, scooped up an oven mitt, and pulled the brownies from the oven. "Perfect timing. The rest of the contestants will be here soon. Ms McCall is outside with Carl setting up for the next challenge."

"And what is it going to be? How many challenges are you doing for this preview?"

"Just three. We had the rodeo thing last week—"

"Uh, that wasn't a rodeo."

"Rodeo... challenge, whatever. Then we have a charity event in a few days. We'd do it sooner, but we can't get the floating lanterns in until the end of this week. But today we're going to do like a kitchen thing. Everyone will be blindfolded, and we're doing a taste test thing. We're going to have to eat things like escargot, pate, and like these mountain grown oyster things."

Emmy scrunched her eyebrows. "You know oysters come from the ocean, right?"

"Duh. But I never knew that they had some in like the lakes up here and stuff." Stacy studied the ceiling. "I wonder what they taste like."

That's because they don't, Emmy thought. What in the world was she talking about? Somewhere in the house, a screen door slammed, causing Emmy to look toward the noise. "I guess we're going to find out in a few minutes."

Stacy held a brownie out to her while she popped one in her own mouth.

"No, thanks." Emmy shook her head, jumped off the

chair, and headed outside. Across the lawn, the two groups of contestants sat in their perspective cliques. The High Heels stood in the shade of a nearby tree, fanning themselves and standing around, one with a scowl while the other chatted happily. Across the lawn, the Cowboy Boots lounged in chairs near rows of tables where people buzzed around, preparing supplies for the next challenge.

"Let's get this thing started!" Stacy yelled to the crowd when she walked out behind Emmy.

The crew jumped to obey Stacy's command, scattering around to complete their tasks. Jax dropped his feet from where he'd lounged with his legs propped onto the back of a chair. He watched her walk across the grass toward him. This was the first time she'd seen him since she'd embarrassingly tried to seduce him. She really wasn't good at these things.

"Contestants," Carl called out, drawing everyone's attention as Stacy made her way through the group, handing out brownies to those who wanted one. "We've paired you up with someone from the opposite team. Some recipes are delicacies that The High Heels are used to, and some of them are right out of the chuck wagon cookbook. You will cook these recipes with your partner. After everyone is finished, we will set you up at the tables blind folded and let you taste each masterpiece. No sharing with the other groups what you've made until after. You all should have noted any food allergies you have, but if we need it, we have a doctor on set to respond." Carl waved toward the table. "Contestants, please come forward. High Heels on this side, and Cowboy Boots on the other. Find your name and the person standing across from you will be your part... ner..." Carl spread his last word out as Stacy ran up to him and whispered in his ear.

He leaned down to respond, and after a short conversation with another crew member who then took off to the tables, he nodded. "Give us one minute, contestants."

Stacy sidled up to Carl and held out a brownie from the tray in her hand. He shook his head and turned back to the crew member who returned with a nod. Carl waved toward the tables. "Contestants, take your places."

Emmy followed Coco as they made their way down the tables, scanning the place cards, and not sure who she wanted to partner with. It's not like she knew any of them. She found her name and picked up the recipe card. Without reading it, she took a stance behind the table and peered up into the humored eyes of the one man on earth she couldn't seem to get out of her mind.

"You know this isn't a coincidence, right?" Jax rounded the table, drawing so close to her she could feel the heat from his body warm the surrounding air. Her heart fluttered. Why did he make her so nervous? It wasn't like he was the first cowboy to talk to her.

"Why do you say that? Why would it be intentional?"

"The guy switched your card around. You were over there." Jax pointed down the table to a station where the contestants opened a lid to reveal what looked like brains.

Emmy choked back the vomit churning in her stomach and burning the back of her throat. "God, I'm glad I'm not there."

"Weren't you paying attention when Carl had that guy come over here?"

"No. I was watching Stacy try to get everyone high before the show."

Jax smirked and raised his chin toward Stacy. "I thought those might be magic brownies."

"Did you eat one?"

"No. You?"

"I've already learned not to partake in things she gives me."

"So what are we making?" Without asking, Jax plucked the recipe from her hand and read it aloud. "After castrating the cow, put the freshly severed testicles in a pot of cold saltwater." Jax pulled the lid off a large pot in the center of their table. "Check."

Emmy raised a single eyebrow and grinned. "I'm pretty sure Stacy thinks Rocky Mountain Oysters are shellfish."

"This is an interesting challenge."

Emmy glanced back to what she thought were calf brains. "I'd say."

Jax followed her line of sight, chuckled, and then dipped his free hand into the testicle water to pull out a handful of meat. He plopped it down on a chopping board as Emmy handed him a towel. After drying his hands, he held the knife out to her. "Do you want to do the honors? You can pretend they're mine if you really want."

She rolled her eyes but took the knife and adjusted a piece of meat.

"It says here to remove the tough membrane and slice 1/4-inch rounds. Slice across the grain."

She pressed the tip of the knife to the meat, and Jax flinched as if she'd pressed it to his crotch instead.

"Wait!" She leaned over his arm and scanned the words. "It says to rinse several times under running water while you cut it to remove the blood."

He glanced around the table. "No running water." He surveyed their surroundings. "We could dip it in the horse trough a few times."

"Gross!" She half laughed and half gagged at the thought, not sure if he was serious or not.

His chest vibrated with a laugh so quiet she wouldn't have

known he gave it except that he was so close she could feel his body move against hers. "You're joking, aren't you?"

"And you're kinda gullible." He set the recipe card down on the table and turned to face her.

"I am not." She defended, but even she didn't believe herself. Truth was, she'd always been a little on the naïve side. Even growing up the way she did, she'd always believed the best of people. Until they'd disappointed her. Much like Stacy had done many times when they were younger, and one of her ex boyfriends had done in her college days. Hence the arrest that almost got her kissed by Stacy herself.

If it wasn't for Emmy's dad warning her about young cowboys, things would have been a lot different back then. As it was, he'd given her enough knowledge to know when she was being played.

Now she stood next to a man she wouldn't mind letting take advantage of her, about to slip the membranes off of a calf testicle.

"Okay, so water. We need water before we cut into this bad boy." She searched for a spigot, but the only one she could see was all the way across the yard near the barn.

"I got it." Jax snapped his fingers and then took off without another word. With nothing else to do, Emmy scanned the recipe for her next steps. Okay. It didn't look too hard. Not much more than making fried chicken at home.

She surveyed the large tub of lard and cast iron pan.

"Except we do it in a boiling pan of heart attack," she murmured to herself.

"That's the best way to make stuff up in the mountains." His shit-eatin' grin returned, and he held out a large plastic pitcher of water. "I'll be your running water. Just watch your shoes." He nodded down to her feet. "Or do you want to take them off for this contest too?"

His eyes shimmered, mimicking his smile, but the look

only added to the already light mood. If he was going to challenge her, tease her, the least she could do was reciprocate.

She quirked up a smile and met his eyes as she kicked off her cowboy boots.

"I wasn't serious. You're wearing boots. Those are perfectly acceptable for this contest." He stared at her like she was crazy, but he kept a smile plastered on his perfect mouth. Damn, she wouldn't mind being kissed by those lips.

She dropped her boots next to his feet. "Now you."

"What?" his smug grin dropped from his face.

"You. Take off your boots. We do this barefoot. Make it interesting."

"Okay," his wolf-like grin grew back on his face and he quickly yanked his boots off. "You are crazy."

"So you've told me."

"Let's do this, my little Bobcat."

JAX YANKED the boots and socks from his feet and let the prickle of the grass ground him to the moment. Emmy didn't know what she did to him. Ever since the first time that he saw her riding in the arena in high school, he knew she was special. He'd watched her every rodeo that year, but never had the guts to approach her.

And when he did, he'd turned into an idiot. She'd made him so nervous that he'd acted like a fool out of defense for his ego. She'd been right to reject him back then, but would she pull away now if he ran his fingers through her hair like he wanted?

God, he wanted to touch the silky smoothness of her hair and feel the auburn tendrils tickle his palm. More than that, he wanted to kiss her, make her see what she'd missed out on all those years ago.

Except as far as he could tell, she still didn't remember him.

Instead, he'd play along with her little game because in all honesty, he loved the way it felt to have her smile at him the way she was right now. It was like they'd been friends for years and never had that distance in time and space between them.

God, he had to get his ridiculous thoughts out of his head. He was a bronc rider, for heaven's sake, not some inexperienced ninny. He'd had more girls fall into his bed than he cared to admit, but none of them were Emmy.

He held the pitcher up. "Ready to slice that poor bastard up?"

"The question is, are you?" She pointed to his crotch, causing him to grow instantly hard. "I saw the way you flinched."

"I am a man," he defended. "But yes. I'm ready."

She prepared the oyster and then picked it up and held it over the grass.

"Watch your toes." He poured the water and then stopped when she returned to the chopping block. "I heard that one time a cook tossed a bag of these out, and the cowboys beat him up so bad for it he almost died."

"That's an overreaction," she mumbled, but smiled. "We need to heat the pan." She motioned with her chin toward the supplies.

He grabbed the cast iron pan off the table and set it over the fire pit that was set up for them to use.

"So are we going to get beat up if we cook these wrong?" she asked when he returned. She held out another piece of meat for rinsing and then continued to prepare it.

"I guess we'll find out."

"I think I can take the High Heels if you got the Cowboy Boots."

He nodded. "I can do that."

There were those dimples again. The ones he wanted to run his thumb over, followed by his lips. Now was as good a time as any to prod Emmy. Get answers to the questions burning in his soul. His stomach bunched with nerves. He didn't care if she did or not, so why did his body feel like it was warming over a fire every time she was close?

"So have you ever been to this part of Montana before?" Let's see if she would tell the truth. Why was she hiding that part about her past, anyway?

"Yeah, once." She ran her gaze across the mountain range before returning to the now stripped and rinsed testicles. "With my godfather."

So she remembered being there, which meant she probably remembered him. "Oh, yeah?"

She battered the oysters. Her eyes flashed with some secret she hid beneath her long lashes. "I guess you can probably tell by now, but I used to barrel race. I even team roped at a county fair with my godfather once."

"You two are close?"

"Closer than me and my mom." She nodded toward Stacy. "Apparently, she set this all up for me. I thought I got the job based on my own merit. Or at least my own connections with Stacy. But it seems my mother set the whole thing up."

"That's not a bad thing. At least she cares about you enough to help you succeed."

"No. There's something else going on. There always is with my mom. And Stacy said there's this mysterious investor. That's sketchy." Emmy tossed a battered ball down. "That's why I would spend the summers and as much time as I could with my godfather."

Jax pointed to her cute little girly cowboy boots. "Those fit you better than those bale hooks you had on the first day you got here."

She kicked the brown and teal leather with her toes. "Yeah, I know."

Her tone told more about her feelings than any words. She regretted something in her life. But what? He doubted it was leaving him on the mountain. She didn't seem to even remember that incident the way he did. "Let's go deep fry these bad boys, and see what Stacy thinks about them."

Emmy picked up a bowl of breaded Rocky Mountain Oysters, and Jax grabbed the lard.

"Careful not to step on an ember. Wouldn't want those pretty toes to get burnt."

She gave him a half-smile. "Thanks."

Jax stepped carefully toward the fire where the cast iron pan smoked, sending off the rich fragrance of heated oil. Cooking next to a campfire barefoot was definitely a first for him. Jax dropped a spoon full of lard into the pan, and it sizzled.

Once it melted, Emmy arranged the Rocky Mountain Oysters inside, and set the rest on a nearby rock. God, she was beautiful. Even covered in flour the way she was, her body radiated a brilliance he'd never seen once on another woman. None of the rodeo bunnies he'd bedded had ever done it for him the way Emmy did. She stood, placed her hands on her hips, and turned toward him, drawing his attention to the way her breasts poked out, begging him to cup.

"I know why I'm here," she said, "but why are you doing this?"

Jax's chest twisted at her question. His reasoning was no one's business but his own, but a strong urge to tell her everything tugged at his core. As though talking to her about it would fix all of his troubles. "You know the story. The ranch has had some bad years. Son comes in to save the family homestead."

"So you did it for the money."

"Didn't you? I know you're the reporter that Stacy hired, aren't you?"

"You know? I didn't think she told anyone that I wasn't anything but a contestant."

"Carl said you were important to this whole thing. I put two and two together. So is that why you came in acting like Stacy's best friend?" He barely knew her, but what he knew was that she was nowhere near the woman she'd pretended to be bouncing down the road in his truck. She was more the one who beat everyone else out of the gate their first contest. The one standing next to a raging fire barefoot cooking steer balls.

Emmy frowned. "I didn't." She watched the other contestants, all going about their business making their chosen dishes. "Okay so maybe I did. I wasn't sure what to expect. New town, new people, new experience. I mean, this is not only my first time being a reality show contestant, but it's my first field job."

"New town? I thought you said you've been here before."

"Oh. Right. Yes. I have, but it was so brief it doesn't count."

He scoffed, snatched up the fire poker, and adjusted the logs. "Boy, you really don't want anyone to know the real Emmy Wilson, do you? You can't even keep up with your own lies right now."

"I'm sorry?" She sounded genuinely confused.

"You seriously don't remember coming here?"

"I mean. Yeah, I remember, but it's complicated."

He tossed the poker down. "You know what? Never mind."

"Look, there's a lot about me people don't know. I'd like to keep it that way. Unlike some of these other contestants, this is a job for me. A way to my success as a person. Not

59

some way to entertain myself during the summer. Yes, I have secrets, but I'd venture to guess that you do too."

"True. You and I are different from most everyone else. We're here for different reasons." He stepped closer to her, forcing her to tip her head back. "That doesn't mean you need to hide the real Emmy Wilson from me."

She held his stare for a moment, her chest rising and falling with her breaths, bringing to mind the low-cut top she'd had on that first day in his truck. Perfection at its finest. But that's not what drew him to her, and made his blood thump through his body as she climbed into his truck.

There was so much about her that drew him in, he couldn't define exactly what made him weak. It was just her. Everything she was.

"What if the show doesn't air? How are you going to save your ranch then?" She lowered her gaze. Did she really care? He hoped so.

Jax took a deep breath to force the mixture of emotions away. Truth was, his plan counted on the show succeeding. Otherwise he had a dicey plan at best. "Either way, we plan to take the money they give us and pay to have our cattle registered. Maybe buy some new rodeo stock. The extra money will keep us afloat until we get established as breeders."

"I hope it works out for you."

The honest tone in her voice both frustrated him and made his stomach drop. Did she really care about him? She didn't in their past. Would it be different now if he tried to kiss her? The way she drew close to him, ran her hand down his arm as she stepped past him to flip the oysters, left him heated and conflicted.

He wanted to hate her. He had for years after he'd walked off the mountain in nothing but his cowboy boots and boxer briefs. He still didn't know what he'd done wrong that night. But he'd give anything to have another shot with her.

She stood tall and smiled at him as though he were the only man in the world. Maybe they could have what they'd missed all those years ago. A new chance at a first love.

## CHAPTER 5

*E*mmy jammed her foot into her boots as she settled into a seat next to Jax while the rest of the contestants took up positions around the long wooden picnic tables set up in the yard. Jax, too, had already slipped his boots on and, to be honest, had shocked the hell out of her when he'd flipped them off his feet. But it was fun. A silly little moment, but one that had lightened her mood and eased the pressure in her chest.

Emmy ran her hand over the red plaid tablecloth. It was so much like the ones her grandma would set out at her dad's ranch. Except here, various condiments sat in the center of each table. Some she'd seen at parties with her mother, and some during dinners at her father's house.

When Jax had asked her if she remembered the town, she'd lied. Obviously. She was an idiot. He was right. She couldn't keep her lies straight anymore. She remembered. It was the first time she'd ever ventured away from the safety of her parents. And the first time she'd ever been tempted to let herself feel passion, to feel anything but regimented order.

She'd wanted to let herself get lost in the boy's arms, but she'd panicked when he'd asked her questions as they shed their clothes and exchanged heated, but awkward kisses. Get to know you questions that were innocent enough conversation, but when mixed with the passion of a teenage affair, had made her nervous.

She'd jumped in the truck she'd come up there in and peeled off down the mountain, leaving him to fend for himself in the woods. She got halfway down the hill before realizing her stupid mistake. She'd gone back for him, but by the time she returned the boy was gone.

It was then that she'd found his clothes in the back of the truck. Along with her flip-flops. So she drove back to the fairgrounds and dumped his truck off next to the grandstands before calling her dad to come pick her up.

It wasn't Jax, though. Right? The boy had been blond and a lot lankier than the dark-haired man before her now. Jax was the sort of man she would remember, right?

Although, he did look a lot like the kid. Maybe relatives? He said his family had settled here. Chances were, it could have been another McCall she'd almost given her virginity away to.

When her dad picked her up, he'd been pissed that she'd disappeared without asking, but she'd needed to be free, at least for a night. She didn't tell him about the boy or stealing his truck. That didn't stop him from threatening to send her back to her mother's for the rest of the year.

After that, she wasn't allowed to compete in any more rodeos. Her punishment for being a regular person for one night. That's when she'd focused on making her own future and doing things that wouldn't depend on her parents for support.

Being her own person. Not caught between two worlds, unable to find herself.

Now, even the condiments screamed at her to choose a side. Why had her mom cared so much about covering up who her father was? She'd never asked why she hated her dad so much, but maybe that was for the best. Her mom had a way of spinning the truth to make herself look like a victim. Her version of things would have probably turned Emmy against her dad, and the only time she'd been truly happy in life was at the ranch.

Next to her, Jax's heat flowed around her and centered in the middle of her core, and for a split second his foot touched hers and sent heat down her leg, causing her breath to freeze in her lungs. She'd never experienced this rush of emotions before. Not even with her college boyfriend, who she'd thought she'd loved at the time.

But with Jax it was different. She couldn't seem to form a rational thought whenever he was around. She'd been programed to keep her wits about her in every situation, to keep certain facts about her childhood from being exposed. But with him, all she wanted to do was talk. She wanted to tell him everything about her, and let him know who she was and every secret she'd kept for all of those years.

There were so many times she had to walk away from a friend or relationship when they'd grown too close or asked too many questions. Then there was the fact that she had to tell everyone she met that she was Tye's goddaughter instead of a biological child. What she wouldn't give to have had a regular childhood.

But she barely knew Jax. And you can't change the past. So she bottled it up inside once more. Only this time, she'd stumbled a little with her lie.

"We have a special treat for you today," Carl called out, bringing the gentle mumble of conversations to a halt and thankfully taking the focus away from her thoughts. "The winners of this contest will receive an all-expense paid trip to the vacation of their choice. We've brought in a very special judge. Contestants, please welcome our newest partner, Rochelle Wilson."

The contestants all murmured excitedly, except Emmy.

Instead, an instant headache formed in the base of her skull. Jax elbowed her while he clapped and motioned toward the cameras that seemed to focus on only her. With a forced smile, she mimicked Jax's rhythm. At least she had him next to her to help her focus on the moment.

Jax leaned in until his breath tickled the base of her neck. "Just keep smiling. It'll be over soon."

"She's got something up her sleeve," Emmy hissed through her teeth as she forced her smile but turned her head toward him until his cheek brushed hers. She heard him suck in a sharp breath before pulling back.

"It's an honor to be here, Carl," her mother's showtime voice echoed through the yard causing Emmy's stomach to drop. What was she up to now? "I see you've all made some delicious-looking dishes here. Fortunately, being the jet setter that I am, I've been all around the world and tasted almost anything I could put in my mouth."

"Oh, good lord," Emmy muttered and struggled not to lean back to hide behind Jax. Panic filled her stomach and flowed up through her chest, causing her breathing to increase. Why hadn't Stacy warned her that her mother was here?

"So, without further ado, let's taste those masterpieces." Cheers erupted as though there were more than just the crew and contestants. That's when Emmy noticed a crew member silencing a sound machine as her mother made her way toward the tables where the dishes were set out.

"Most of you know my daughter is a contestant here, but don't worry. Carl has made it so I don't know which dish is hers." Her mother smiled at her as though they were best friends. Which they weren't. Emmy had lived mostly in Montana. She'd spent as much time there as possible and only came out so that her mother could show her off.

Not that her mom had cared. When she talked about being a jet setter, she wasn't kidding. Half of the time Emmy spent with her they'd been flying to some corner of the world, either filming a movie or taking a vacation. It was rare to have nothing going on when she was with her mother.

"Should we go over there?" Jax asked, drawing close to her. His closeness calmed her down just a little.

"Do you really want to taste bull balls and calf brains today? Plus, I'm pretty sure one group had escargot. I already know I'm not a fan."

"Okay then." A mysterious glint shined from the center of Jax's eyes. "I've got a better idea. You wanna go somewhere? I know a place no one will find you until you want them to." He ran his gaze around the crowd. "We'll have to act fast to shake the cameras."

"And my mother." Emmy glanced around, but all the cameras and crew were centered on her mom. "Hell yeah. Let's go."

Without another word, Jax jumped up, grabbed Emmy's hand, and ran toward his truck. The knot in her chest lightened with each freeing step. Her breath came at even intervals, and her fingers tingled with excitement. She'd only ever run away like this once. All those years ago when she'd wanted desperately to be normal—wild and carefree. It had come back to bite her in the ass, but she had to believe that today would be different.

For one, she was with Jax.

She jumped into the truck and slammed the door as he turned the key. "You just keep your keys in your unlocked truck, huh?"

"Who's going to steal it all the way out here besides you?" Jax peeled out of the driveway and headed down the dirt road. Emmy turned and peered out the window at the dirt cloud behind them, but no second vehicle followed.

They'd escaped. At least she had a small reprieve from her mother.

"True." The road opened up before her, thinning as it stretched and disappearing into the mountainside before her. "Why did you help me?"

He gave her a sideways glance. "You looked like you needed rescuing. I wasn't about to leave a damsel in distress."

"Thanks." She meant it. No one had ever helped her escape except the rodeo queen and her friends, who Emmy suspected might just be Jax. What would that mean if it was? Did he hate her for leaving him on the mountain? "Where are we going?"

"The North 40. I have a spot there that no one knows about." He slowed down as he turned a curve in the road.

"You trust me with your secret?" She cricked half her mouth up in a teasing grin.

"You've got so many of them. I think one more would just get lost inside that pretty little brain of yours."

She reached up and smoothed her hair against her scalp. "So what you're saying is you like a woman with brains before beauty?"

"Why not both?"

"Men don't want both. It's just not a thing."

"Why not?"

Emmy watched the scenery pass the window as Jax's truck climbed a hill. In her limited experience, they either wanted one or the other. Never both. "They just don't. They either expect you are dimwitted and slutty, or smart and a prude."

"But you're not like that."

Emmy blinked at his tone. It wasn't a question, but a statement. It was like he knew her better than she thought, even though they'd only known each other a week.

She perused his body as he drove. Damn, he was sexy. If a man like him wants a woman like her, you go for it. No questions asked. Problem was, he could have any woman at the ranch right now. There was no way he would go start some meaningless fling with her. And even if he did, how many other contestants had he slept with already?

Okay, maybe very few. If at all. She'd mostly seen him working, not sneaking behind the barn with some chick. She'd even seen him reject Stacy's advances a few times in the barn before he noticed her and walked away. "Have you been avoiding me this last week?"

"Nope. Just busy taking care of things."

"Are you sure?" Somehow, she doubted he would tell her even if she begged. Best leave it alone and take his word for it. "Where are we going?"

"To get you out of your boots again."

"Oh, yeah?" Her heart lightened at his playful tone. She wasn't sure what to make of the comment, but whatever he meant she knew she would have fun doing it. This time there was no voice in the back of her mind nagging at her to: *come home, be a good girl, protect the family secret.*

No. Right now was all about her and what she wanted to do.

And she wanted to do Jax.

JAX PARKED his truck in the usual spot near his favorite swimming hole. He wasn't sure why he'd jumped at the chance to run away from the chaos below, but he was glad he did. He liked the way her face lit up when he'd turned that second corner. As if he'd given her a gift she'd wanted all of her life.

He knew she had secrets, but what had her mother done to her that running away for an hour or so could make her so happy?

She tipped the sexiest smile he'd ever seen his way. "You said no shoes. Are we going swimming?"

"Is that what you want to do?" His heartbeat kicked up at the thought. And if he was lucky, they would be naked. His body responded instantly to the thought of Emmy bare for him to enjoy, passion dusting her skin, and raw need flowing off her like the ripples on the water. Did she have tan lines or not? Either way, it didn't matter. He knew she would be flawless. "I'd thought more like dipping our feet in, but swimming is good too."

Jax shook the thought free. He didn't want to start something with Emmy. She'd probably steal his truck and run away again.

Then again, it might be worth it. As long as she ran after they made love and not before.

Love. He scoffed. That didn't exist. He'd been in enough failed relationships, and a few no-strings attached hookups, to know that a man like him didn't find that one perfect person. Or at least a man like the one he'd been trying to shake didn't. The kind that made out with Stacy Siepres just for the hell of it. The man he'd been trying to replace ever since he learned that the future of the ranch was in jeopardy. He had to grow up. And that's what he was doing. Then again, his dad had told him on more than one occasion that he wouldn't grow up until he stopped riding the circuit.

But Emmy was already there, already the responsible adult one would expect at their age. She was everything he wasn't.

Which was what he needed, but with a woman like

Emmy, probably not what he would get. He'd settle for having this moment with her, though.

"Come on, Cowboy. Let's do this." The excitement in her voice was infectious. Jax jumped from the truck, trying to maintain an air of ease as he followed her to the swimming hole.

She twirled as she walked, taking in the view with a smile on her face he'd never seen her have before. "You like it here, I take it?"

"I feel…" she cast her eyes toward the sky as if searching the clouds for her next words. "I feel light. Happy."

She once again slipped her cowboy boots off and arranged them by the bank. Blood rushed straight to his groin when she yanked her shirt off, followed closely by her tight, hip-hugging jeans, and then tiptoed into the water, not caring if anyone saw her mismatching underwear. God, she was cute. Perfect, like he remembered. He had only gotten her top off back then, but it had been enough to let him know he'd never see another woman as flawless as her. At least to him she was.

"Come on." She swirled the top of the water, causing ripples to spread out and disappear into the surface. "I thought we were swimming."

He swallowed hard while he searched the haze in his brain for what to say. All he wanted to do was rush into the water, take her into his arms and show her what it was they could have had all those years ago.

His jeans grew uncomfortably tight, and he resisted the urge to adjust himself as he watched her stare at him as if she wanted to devour him. If he took off his pants now, there would be no hiding what she'd done to him.

"I'll just enjoy the show from here." The roughness in his voice gave away his problem. There was no hiding it. What he should have done was walk away and keep his distance while she enjoyed the freedom she so desperately needed.

But he couldn't move. Couldn't speak.

Before he could say anything else, she walked out of the water like a siren drawing in her next victim. She could have him. He'd been hers for years. He knew that now.

He struggled to keep his breath easy, not wanting her to know just how much she affected him. It wasn't until she reached him, stood on her tiptoes, and kissed him that he let his restraint go.

Her lips pressed against his and all he could concentrate on was how she tasted and the way her breasts felt against his body. He reached up and cupped her face in his hands, not wanting to let her go. Afraid she might run again. Afraid she might pull away.

Instead, he felt a gentle tug at his belt buckle, and whatever reins he had on his control snapped. She finished with his belt and tugged at the waist of his jeans, so he kicked off his boots, slipped his pants and boxer briefs past his hips, and admired the way the water drops pooled in the hollow of her clavicle.

Droplets cascaded down her face when he pulled his head back to let her yank his shirt over his head. All he could handle was a few seconds without her kiss, so he quickly took her mouth again, this time reaching down to cup her buttocks and lift her up.

In sync with him, she wrapped her legs around his waist as he carried her into the water, still savoring the way her lips opened and her tongue flicked against his teeth. Driving him even more crazy.

Submerged up to their chests, he juggled her until he could free one hand and then tugged the cups on her bra down. Her breasts sprang free, and he immediately dipped his head to suck one nub into his mouth, followed by another. He groaned in appreciation when she arched her back, pressing against his mouth even more. "God, baby, you're so hot."

"Jax," she moaned, her voice breathless and filled with passion.

He should stop this. Or at least rush to his truck and get protection. But he couldn't leave her arms. Afraid she'd come to her senses and realize again how much better she could do than him. Afraid that distance, no matter how small, would shatter the moment.

"It's not fair that I'm naked and you're not," he said between kisses, and he trailed them up her collar bone and jaw, only to return to her mouth.

Without breaking the connection between their lips, she wiggled free and slipped her underwear off. In a moment, her bra floated free from her body.

"This is your last chance to run, Bobcat. But…" He picked her up again, and she straddled him once more. He adjusted himself along the crease in her thigh. "Please don't go."

She responded by reaching between them and sitting straight down onto him.

The sensation of her hot heat hit him like a punch to the gut that he wanted to experience again and again. He moved his hips, and she picked up his rhythm with ease. He trailed his kisses from her mouth, down her neck, stopping briefly at her shoulder.

With her head suspended above him, she dropped her chin until she caught his stare. The passion in her eyes mirrored his own. Could this be real? Could he really be living the fantasy he'd had since she'd first rejected him?

He dropped his gaze to her mouth. Plump and pink with lines that fanned out to accentuate the passion swollen lips. All he could think about was the taste of her and the way she felt as she rode him harder than a bronc fresh off of the range.

She leaned back again, her hair dipping into the water as she exposed her chest enjoying the way he drove her on. He ran his free hand down the center of her body from the base of her neck, all the way to where they connected.

Her breaths came in rapid succession. She was near the edge, and knowing it made him even harder inside of her. Fuck. If she explodes around him, he didn't think he could hold back himself. Hell, just thinking about it brought him to the edge.

His breaths grew as desperate as hers as he pumped harder, pushing her to the edge and wanting to see the way her skin flushed when she came.

He clutched her hips with both hands now, anchoring her while he used the water to help him thrust into her as hard as he could until her waves of ecstasy cascaded around him and he released himself deep inside her.

He didn't want to move. Didn't want to shatter the moment. He dropped his head against her chest and took a deep breath as he waited for the lovers high to ebb.

Once her breaths slowed to match his own, she wiggled free. Reluctantly, he dropped his hold on her and let her go. Needing the cool of the water to bring him fully back, he submerged his face in the water and let the cool breeze bring his focus back to the present. "I'm sorry. I shouldn't have done that without protection."

"I'm on the pill. Wait... you don't have anything I should know about, do you? I mean, I don't know how many girls you've been with, but I'm assuming I'm not the first."

"No. You're safe." He knew he sounded disgusted but couldn't help it. He'd been with his fair share of women, but this was honestly the first time he'd done so without protection. And he wasn't a man whore.

Emmy was different. She was the woman he wanted to see full of his babies. The woman he wanted to smile at from across the table and see her grey hair and wrinkles beside her eyes.

He wanted her to love him the way he now realized he'd been in love with for all of those years.

## CHAPTER 6

*E*mmy clutched her cell phone and searched the shadows of the barn, hoping to find a spot to be alone. She had to figure out what she'd experienced with Jax yesterday. Sex, yes. But something more. She'd never felt that way before. If she'd been searching for the freedom to just be her, she found it at the swimming hole. Now, all she could think about was the way he felt deep inside her, tugging her chord of ecstasy until it snapped. He captured her with the look in his eyes, one of possession, need, and something else. Something deeper.

After they had come down from the high, they'd dressed and rolled down the mountain, not sure what to say to each other. At least that's how she felt. The confusion in his expression made her believe he felt it, too.

Once they got back, night shrouded the land, and she slipped into her bed and feigned sleep when Stacy and the rest of the High Heels clamored into the bunkhouse drunk.

Now she tried hard to avoid everyone. Especially Jax and her mother.

A noise near the entrance to the barn caught her attention as her mother picked her way inside in expensive heels. "Emmy! Emmy!"

Emmy sighed. "I'm over here."

"Where the hell have you been? Do you know how embarrassing it was to see you running away with that cowboy while I was supposed to be making my announcement? When the cameras cut to you, all they saw was your ass jumping into a filthy truck. And you won the vacation, but you weren't even there to accept the prize. You embarrassed me."

"Sorry, Mom. You caught me off guard. I needed to work through everything Stacy just told me and seeing you." Emmy waved toward where the spectacle had been outside the barn the day before. What she should do is tell her mother where to shove her microphone.

"Listen, this thing is big for my career. Do not screw this up for me. You only have to get through tomorrow's party, and then you can go back to New York and write the article. I'll make sure you get the material to make it amazing."

Emmy grimaced. "Big for your career? Isn't this Stacy's thing?"

Her mom laughed. "Dear. Please. Stacy couldn't think of something like this. I'm the one who orchestrated it all." Her mom shrugged. "Stacy was just looking for something to do to turn her image around. So I gave it to her. We agreed to help each other out. I convinced her father to give it a chance, and I invested in part of it. I had you brought here. It's as much about us as it is her."

Emmy switched her phone into the other hand and crossed her arms. "Why do you need Stacy's project? You're Rochelle Wilson."

Her mom gave a frustrated sigh. "My career is slowing down." She spread her arms out as she spoke. "My last audition was for the part of the grandma in a low budget film, Emmy. The grandmother. Do you know how embarrassing that is? I'm past old as far as my world sees it. I'm here to spark another flame, and Stacy is where it's at these days."

"One last attempt to stay relevant?" Emmy rolled her eyes and shook her head. Figures she'd pull something like this. "So you can't even make it to my college graduation, but you'll pull out the stops for a reality show that may not even air?"

"Oh, it will air. I've already made the arrangements for Stacy's dad to pick it up."

"Great. You have everything you need. So why bring me here?"

"Oh. My, dear." Her mother stepped toward her and pulled Emmy's hair out from behind her ear to arrange it over her shoulder, smoothing the tendrils. "We're family. People need to see us do this together."

"I still don't understand how this will resurrect your career."

"You will soon enough." Her mom's phone dinged, and she checked the screen. "I have to take this. Just act excited tomorrow at the party, please?"

Her mother walked away, but before she could leave the barn, Emmy shouted, "You know I'm not doing a whole season of this, right?"

Her mother waved in response as Emmy's phone rang. Relief spread through her chest when Marissa's name popped onto the screen. "Hello."

"This guy you texted me about, is he Mel Gibson cute, or more like Brad Pitt?" Marissa asked from the other side of the phone line.

"Showing your age there, Marissa." Emmy held her breath as the memory of the way Jax stared at her as if he could see right into her soul. Of how he'd lifted her up with ease and made everything feel right. What was it about him that seemed so familiar?

He'd made a few comments that brought back memories, but that had to be a coincidence, right? She would remember if she'd have met a cowboy like Jax in the past. Wouldn't she? "He's somewhere in the middle. He's extremely considerate but as conceited as a bull rider. He says he rides broncs, so I guess that's about right."

"Oh my God, you hussy. You had sex with him. Tell me all about it."

"The world shook. Okay. That's all I'm going to say."

"That bad, huh? Well, at least he's cute."

Emmy quietly chuckled.

"Look. Don't fall in love with him," Marissa said. "Just have some fun, and then come home in a few days. You need this, Emmy. You're all tight skirts and business. You need to be daisy dukes and Jimmy Choo's like Stacy. Maybe not as bad as her, but you could let her wear off on you a little. Enough to come out to *The Urban Cowboy* with me when you get home."

"I'll come to that dive bar when real cowboys ride the bull."

"Oh yeah? I'll take your word on that. I think the pro bull riding thingy is coming to town sometime this year. Maybe I can convince a few of those arrogant asses to come party."

"It won't be hard. I'm pretty sure drinking, fighting, and loving is a bull rider's motto." Emmy picked at the peeling red barn paint as she hid in the back corner of the dust-filled building.

"Did you get the angle for the story yet?" She could hear Marissa turn on the bath water. What she wouldn't give to be back home and relaxing alone in her old, and very used, claw-foot tub.

"Sort of. It's all falling into place." She didn't tell her

friend that the whole thing had been staged. Orchestrated by her mother.

Marissa mumbled something into the receiver, but Emmy didn't hear. Her concentration snapped to Stacy's voice floating in through the large barn doors. "No silly, I want you to show me how to ride. It's hard."

"I gotta go, Rissa," she whispered into the receiver, and spun around to watch the large door.

"See ya. Call me tomorrow." Marissa's phone clicked off as Stacy, Jax, and his friend Chase walked into the barn.

"I thought we'd find you here." Jax said, his voice easy but not as sensual and raw as by the swimming hole. The way his hand felt sliding down her hip replayed in her mind, and heat flowed to every inch of her body.

She was stupid. Stupid and well satisfied. *Just get the story and get home,* she chided herself. She didn't have room for a relationship right now. Not with a cowboy like Jax. Her lips tingled at the memory of his kisses.

One more kiss wouldn't hurt, right?

"Oh, Emmy!" Stacy grabbed Jax's hand and flounced toward her, towing him behind. "Jax was about to give me a riding lesson. Of course, you don't need one. You already know. You like went to live with your godfather in Montana whenever your mom was gone filming, right?" Stacy rubbed her boobs—now bedecked in a diamond-encrusted bikini top—against Jax's side. She knew damn well her godfather was her dad, but at least Stacy was keeping up Emmy's family lie for them. Then again, she too had ulterior motives. Stacy smiled. "That's why Emmy is so good at riding. I made a good call bringing her on our team."

"Is this show even going to air?" Emmy sure as hell hoped not. Then again, her mother had promised to make it happen. And mom always got her way.

"It will if I have anything to say about it." Stacy perked up.

79

"This is my baby. I want to be a producer, and this is my way in. You will come back to compete for real if this goes forward, right Emmy?"

Crap! She didn't want to say no and piss the woman off, but there was no way in hell she would spend any more time in the show than needed. "Maybe."

"You better." Stacy's top rubbed against Jax's arm, and he flinched.

Was it bad of Emmy to hope the diamonds were as uncomfortable as they looked? Was it bad of her to want to be the only woman to lean into Jax? It wasn't like she had an actual claim on him. She had no right to be jealous.

"I mean riding is great, especially when you get the rhythm down perfect." Jax stared at her. His eyes fired with the same passion she'd seen in them before and caused her breath to catch when he continued. "I'll bet I could show you a few tricks, Emmy. If you're up for another ride."

He studied her from her face to her toes, stopping briefly at her boobs. *Hell, yes!* Her mind screamed, but her more logical side took over. In a forced, cheerful voice she responded with, "That would be nice. Thank you."

What was wrong with her? Other than wanting to feel his body pressed against hers once more. Holy crap, it was like she'd never made love to a man before.

I mean, she had, but it had never been like it was with Jax.

"I'm sure you learned so much on all of your previous ponies," he teased, rising a single eyebrow. "We could take the high trail and I'll show you some more advanced techniques."

"I don't know. I have a lot to do here. I have to write the article, and my mother..." she let the rest go unsaid, mostly to seem a little mysterious. Not at all as excited as she actually felt. She wanted to make the other people in the barn disappear and yank Jax on top of her in the hay in the corner of the barn. When he raised a single eyebrow, she smiled. "I guess I could come. I'm not as experienced as you are, though. Are you sure the high trail is right for me?"

What was she doing? Challenging him for no good reason. She wanted to take the high trail. What hot blooded woman wouldn't with a man like Jax.

"I'm going on Misty Morning," Stacy interrupted, oblivious to the real meaning behind their conversation. "Jax said it was a white mare. Isn't that what you said?"

Jax kept his eyes on Emmy, ignoring Stacy. "You're plenty experienced."

She returned his stare, lifted one brow, and lowered her head the slightest bit in a silent challenge. Her pulse sped up, and her mouth flooded with moisture as another round of memories flowed through her mind.

Lust sparkled in the depths of his eyes, but he remained silent. Why did she want to spar with him so bad? In more than the verbal way.

He slid out of Stacy's clutch and shifted closer so that she had to crane her head back to peer up at his tanned face. God he was sexy. His lips curled back in that smile that made a wolf look friendly. "It's a date then. I'll take you up the high trail to Snowy Pond."

She lifted her head and studied him with what she hoped was an equally wolfish stare. "I never said I'd go."

"Chicken," he taunted.

Stacy shifted closer to her, reminding her to keep up appearances. She tilted her head to the side like a pup listening to a noise and mimicked Stacy's sensual tone from earlier. "I'd love to ride your horse."

"Okay, wait." Stacy pointed at the two of them. "What's going on here?"

Chase stepped up next to Stacy and dropped his arm around her shoulders. "I think they're settling an old score. Come on. I'll help you get that horse ready."

Jax gave his signature wolf grin and lowered his head until she could feel his hot breath tickle her lips. Her stomach churned, and a tingle prickled down from her core to her toes, threatening to take away the strength in her legs. Jax took a deep, slow breath and slid his gaze to her mouth. "We've got the night free. How about right now?"

"What about me?" Stacy whined from where she stood next to a stall, drawing the attention of everyone in the barn. "Can we at least go on our horse ride first?"

Jax's demeanor changed at her words. Humor shined in his eyes, and he raised his eyebrows so only Emmy could see. He sobered and turned toward the horses. "It's a tough ride. I don't know if you can handle it."

"I can." Stacy popped her hip out. "I can handle it as long as you give me the good horse."

Jax scratched his face. His tone, however, was no longer playful and oozing with sexuality. "There are plenty of horses to go around, and the best way to learn is to get on and go. Chase will get you set up with a nice little mare, and then we'll head up the hill." He turned back to Emmy, a twinkle of mischief shining in his eyes. "I think Jake is good for you, Bobcat. If you're game."

"Lead on." No way was she going to let Stacy ride up into the mountains alone with Jax and Chase. She wouldn't doubt if Stacy tried to have a threesome up there. Not that Emmy could claim Jax for her own. She'd only made love to him once, but that didn't mean she couldn't be jealous enough to care.

He waved toward the row of horses further down the barn. "After you."

Emmy knew he aimed to check out her ass as she walked by. Any man with a shit eatin' grin and cowboy hat would, so she swayed just enough to give him a tease.

Marissa was right. She was a hussy. But only for Jax.

THE TERM high strung fit Jake the horse to a tee, but even with his intense power Emmy had no problem handling him. And the mark on his face made an ache start in the pit of her stomach and spread to her heart. It looked so much like Butterscotch, her barrel racing horse that she'd had as a teen. She'd loved her horse just as much as she'd loved being with her father.

Now here she was, riding behind a man so perfect that he was the prime example of the man her father had told her to avoid. And she couldn't stop wanting him.

Frankly, she couldn't believe Jax hadn't already figured out one of her many secrets. Or had he? Maybe that's what all the looks were about. Maybe he knew.

He was the sort of man who idolized professional bronc riders like her dad. Chances were, in his life, Jax owned a poster of her cowboy famous father.

Hmm... her thoughts drifted to Jax's bedroom. What did it look like? Would she ever find out? Doubtful. This was a summer thing. Nothing else. She wasn't in love with him, and he wasn't in love with her. He probably had every woman in the valley falling at his feet.

The horse's muscles rippled beneath her thighs—the power beneath the twitching skin unmistakable with each lunge up the steep incline. He was a beauty, a tall and sleek sorrel with a star on his forehead, snip on his nose, and three socks. She admired his independence and free spirit fighting to be released from captivity.

Emmy crested the top of the treacherous hill and stopped Jake for a breather as they waited for the others to catch up. Jax was already there. But Chase had opted to drop behind to help Stacy.

"Go ahead," Chase shouted. "Stacy wants to take a break. We'll meet up with you later."

Jax nodded and kicked his horse.

"You shouldn't have brought Stacy along. She's never ridden before," she chastised him when they drew far enough away to not be overheard.

"Yeah." He scoffed toward where the other riders eased around a bend in the treacherous trail. "Plus, I can't see how you look naked in the patch of fireweed that grows up there." He patted a saddlebag behind him. "I even brought a blanket."

"Oh, how romantic." She smiled playfully.

"I was going to see if I could get your nipples to peak using nothing but a flower."

"Not your tongue?" She dropped her chin and peered at him sideways, allowing a lustful grin to stretch across her face.

He responded by shaking his head. "You're an amazing woman. You know that? A woman like you could be dangerous for a man. How did you do it?"

"Do what?"

"Get this far without being snatched up by some mook in the city."

"I have my secrets." She kicked her horse to urge him up a steep incline. "I'm sure you have things you don't want people to know."

"Not me. I'm as open as the Great Plains." He raised his chin toward the trail before them. "The meadow is just over the hill."

They rode silently for the rest of the trail until they rounded a bend that opened up to a rich, green meadow so serene it stole her breath. She slipped from the saddle. "Gorgeous, but I thought you were taking me to a pond."

"This is Snowy Pond Meadow." When she gave him a curious stare, he chuckled. "Don't ask."

"Let me guess, your family named this meadow too."

He yanked his cowboy hat off and scratched the back of his head. "Gotta keep things interesting."

"With weird names?"

"And apparently by bringing film crews in to do shows that might or might not help the ranch the way we need it to."

Emmy walked to a nearby boulder and settled on top, the surrounding scene vaguely familiar. "Why did you sign up for this, anyway?"

"Ah, Ms. Emmy. You don't want to hear about my family's troubles."

"I mean. I do, but I didn't mean to pry." She held out her hands in surrender.

"You're not prying. My family's problems are a known thing around these parts." He plucked a tall blade of grass out of the ground, snapped the top off, and tossed it.

"Anything I can do to help?"

"Who are you, Emmy Wilson?" he asked, changing the subject. "I don't know any rich kids who can ride western and handle Jake the way you do. I know you grew up with your godfather, but even then. Most people like you don't care about people like me, and here you are offering to help."

She tried hard not to wiggle beneath his penetrating stare. She wanted to tell him her secret. Desperately wanted to, but doing so was out of the question. Like Stacy at the beginning of the show, Emmy had been forced to sign a legal agreement when she left the house. She wouldn't tell anyone who her father was. Why her mother cared so much about keeping his identity a secret was beyond her. "I'm Emmy Wilson, daughter of Rochelle Wilson."

"That's not what I mean."

Her heart started to beat so hard she had to swallow to

keep it from jumping straight into her throat. "I'm no one special."

"Look. We only have a few minutes before Chase and Stacy get up here." He ran a nervous glance to the trailhead, and then back at Emmy, causing her stomach to flip. "I just… I wanted to ask you. Do you seriously not remember me?" He squared his body to hers. "Remember us?"

"I mean. You seem familiar. This place does too, but where would I remember you from?"

"Right here." He pointed over to an area just off the regular path. The charred remains of a well-used fire pit blackened the ground in the center of what looked to be a regularly used camp. "I brought you up in my old brown truck. The one you stole."

"That was here?" The memories of the night she'd snuck away from her father to party with the local cowboys surfaced again. Honestly, she'd been to so many rodeos that year she didn't know which town she'd been at when she snuck away. And the boy she'd almost given herself to looked so different from Jax. It had been so many years ago, and dark out. She ran through her memories of that night.

She'd let herself go at first and enjoyed the moment of freedom. But then guilt and her mother's voice niggled at the back of her mind, berating and screaming at her until she'd ran down the hill with the boy's truck leaving him with nothing but his boots, boxers, and wounded pride.

"You're not that Jaxson? The one with the ten-gallon hat, blonde hair, and chain wallet."

"Yes, I am. But in my defense, everyone had a chain wallet back then. Even here in small town Montana."

Emmy bit the tip of her thumb as the vague memories of that night filtered past. She'd been relaxing in her shorts and flip-flops when a few of the barrel racers invited her out for some after rodeo riding. They'd been back at the arena for maybe thirty minutes when a truck full of boys pulled up to invite them to a party in the mountains. Before she had a chance to ask her father, she put her horse away and jumped in the nearest truck. They were halfway up the mountain by the time she looked back. Her father hadn't a clue she was missing until later that night when he'd come back to the fairgrounds to find her, expecting her to be riding.

The guilt had eaten at her all night, but she didn't want to leave. It wasn't until most of the group trickled out of camp in various other vehicles that she'd realized what exactly she'd done. And then Jaxson had kissed her.

Back then it had been… well, not as good as it was now. She chalked it up to inexperience. Back then it had been more about getting his tongue in her mouth. Now he worked his kisses like a skillful art, teasing and tempting, drawing her on and making her want more.

She'd run away, both from the guilt eating away at her insides and because of the intense feelings driving her to the edge, demanding she give herself away for the first time to a boy she'd only met hours before.

Now she felt guilty for a whole new reason. "How did you get home?"

"I walked."

"All the way down the mountain?"

"I got about halfway before Chase found me and took me home. In my underwear."

She lowered her eyes to the tip of her boots. "I came back for you, you know. But you were gone."

"You did?"

"Yeah."

He tossed down the blade of grass and plucked another one. "Why'd you leave like that? Did I do something?"

"No. It's just…" she paused and searched for the right way to explain. "I was young and naïve. New to all of this socializing stuff. Before then, the only people I'd ever been allowed to hang out with was my da… godfather's ranch hand's kids, and Stacy." She gave a sardonic chuckle. "And you can imagine I didn't like hanging out at the Siepres house."

"So you were pretty sheltered, huh? You'd think as a rich kid you would have more life experience than us out here in the country."

"My parents differed from most."

"Like how?"

Emmy chewed on her bottom lip, debating about how much to tell him. "Well, for one, when I wasn't at the ranch, I mostly was on the road with mom."

"What about school?"

"I was homeschooled. Well, actually I had a tutor that would go with me wherever I went. That's one reason I joined the NHSRA. I wanted to meet people my age." Emmy flicked him a nervous glance, worried he'd ask more than she was allowed to say. "And for another, I couldn't talk about who my father is. I still can't."

Jax raised both eyebrows. "That can't be easy, keeping a secret like that your whole life."

"Trust me. It's not."

"That explains a lot about you."

She stood and dusted off her backside, needing to pace. "What do you mean?"

She took a few steps then flipped around, only to run straight into Jax's chest. He caught her in his arms, and she instantly relaxed, comforted by the warmth of his body.

"It explains why you're so mysterious." He tipped his hat up with his index finger. "Why you're so good at keeping secrets, and why you fit so perfectly into both worlds in this whole competition thing."

She closed her eyes and then peered back up at him. "And why I left you that night. I'm sorry. I'd never been to a party before." She waved toward the cold fire pit. "Not one like this, anyway. And I was a virgin back then. I was scared."

"You're not scared of me now." He lowered his head until his lips barely brushed hers.

"No," she whispered into his breath a mere second before he kissed her.

This kiss differed from the ones by the swimming hole. Those were needy and raw, filled with unbridled passion. This one was tender, sweet, and gentle like he wanted her to know she could trust him. But she already knew that. They'd only spent a few weeks together at the ranch, but somehow deep inside she knew. She didn't want to lose what they'd just discovered.

## CHAPTER 7

"What are you doing here, Dad?" Emmy didn't mean for her words to sound rude, but her entire world—well, both of her worlds—had just come crashing down when her dad stepped out of his one-ton Ford. Cars surrounded them and several pulled in to park, headed for the charity party. By the looks of them, they were local. Although the occasional Bentley or Mercedes took up space in the dusty ranch driveway. Behind her father's truck, a horse trailer shook when the animal within stomped and whinnied.

What was her dad doing here?

Then again, he fit in better in this world than her mother did. What was she doing here? Emmy's stomach dropped when the shimmer of a blue sequined gown caught her attention as her mother stepped gingerly from the front porch of the main house.

"Don't get your back up. They invited me," her dad said.

Emmy crossed her arms over her red cocktail dress as the vision of the shit storm that was about to hit smacked her brain. Her mother would not be happy. She'd spent every year of Emmy's childhood avoiding any one-on-one time with her father. "Invited by who?"

"By me." Her mother stopped next to her.

"Why?" Nothing good could come of this. Emmy balanced on her heels.

"You'll see, darling." Emmy's mom looped her arm through her father's and plastered a warm smile on her face —as if they were old friends.

She turned to her dad. "Do you know what's going on?"

He nodded. "I do."

"Then what?"

"I can't say, Pumpkin." Her father used the nickname he'd always gave when trying to calm her down. This time it would not work.

Her stomach churned, and her chest tightened. She struggled to take in deep breaths. All the years of secrets, all the times she'd walked away from friends because they grew too close, too curious. Now, when she's at the verge of making it on her own without them and their drama interfering, they caused drama. All because, what? Her mother needed to get her career back on track? She couldn't find a better, less intrusive way to do so?

Rochelle Wilson had always been the driving force behind their family issues. I mean, heaven forbid anyone know she'd had a fling with a cowboy and as a result, a bastard child.

Not that her childhood had been bad. She'd always been fed and clothed. Always had a home—two of them, really. Emmy had always gotten everything she'd wanted. Except a regular childhood.

"Look, Pumpkin. We can't say anything right now. We signed one of those confidentiality things," her father said.

"But you'll know everything soon enough. Promise." Her mother smoothed Emmy's hair and pulled a chunk to lie on her shoulder. A move she'd always done when showing her affection.

"Yeah? When?" She really didn't need to ask the question. She knew the answer.

While the cameras were rolling.

"Soon. The party is about to start, and we should get inside before anyone sees your father." Her mother tugged on her dad's arm.

"I've got to tend to the horses and find the guy who bought the gelding," he argued.

Her mother waved toward the expanse of the ranch. "They've got people for that."

"A good cowboy doesn't let another man care for his horse."

"It isn't your horse anymore," her mother pointed out.

"Still." Her father took a step toward the trailer.

"Fine." Her mother huffed. "Emmy can take care of the horse. We need to get inside. Carl has been waiting for you."

"Hey, Pumpkin." Her father said. "Do you mind? There's hay in the trailer."

Emmy smoothed her eyebrow and closed her eyes. No good could come of tonight. "No problem, Dad. I got it."

She waited for her parents to escape into the house and then made her way to the trailer. She didn't mind taking care of the horse for her dad. It would give her a familiar task to do while working through the implications of her father showing up.

She lowered the back door and stepped wobbly inside.

Damn it! She hated wearing heels! If the party had been a different affair, she'd have settled for her boots. But no. Tonight was all about fashion and sophistication.

The horse snorted and sidestepped, so she held out her hand for the animal to smell and crooned. "Whoa, boy. It's okay."

After the horse settled, she untied to lead rope.

"Do you want me to help you take your shoes off?" Jax's voice sounded from the doorway to the trailer.

Emmy spun around. "Funny. But these stay on tonight."

Jax sighed and shook his head. "Shame. I love watching you frolic around the ranch like a hooligan."

"I don't know any hooligans who run around dressed in designer dresses." She ran a critical eye over him. Instead of the usual blue jean and T-shirt look he usually sported, Jax stood in a suit that made him look like he belonged on Wall Street... well, except for the newly shinned, but well used, cowboy boots.

She bit her lip to stop the smile from creeping on her face, but he must have noticed. He shuffled his feet. "The loafers they gave me pinched."

"You look nice."

"I look like a dandy."

She raised one eyebrow. "A dandy?"

"Yeah. The city guys who come out here to play cowboy during a work retreat." He shrugged. "Dandies."

She smiled and urged the horse to back out of the trailer.

"Here, let me." He took the lead rope from her. "Wouldn't want you tripping on your bale hooks and spooking my new stud."

"Your new horse?"

"Yes, ma'am."

"You bought a horse?"

"Sort of. I convinced Carl to let me trade in my vacation for a horse."

"How d'you do that?"

"I think Stacy had something to do with it. She's not as bad as she seems."

"You didn't want to get an all expense paid trip to wherever you want?"

"Anywhere I go I can pay for myself. And if I can't afford it myself, I figure I don't really need to go there. A horse I need. So that's my Plan B: breeding horses with a quality stud."

"Plan B?" She walked next to him as he led the horse to the barn. "It doesn't sound too solid."

"I will breed him with my dad's roping horse. Try to get a few pro guys buying up my stock. Maybe I'll eventually get a line of rough stock."

"So plan A is hosting the show and buying the cattle, and Plan B is the horse?"

"I know. It's not much to go on, but it's better than sitting here and watching the ranch sink. If the show doesn't air, then at least I have the stud to breed with our mares."

"I hope it all works out for you." Her phone beeped, and Emmy checked as her mother's text flashed across the screen. "We need to get inside. They're about to start."

Jax finished securing the horse while Emmy tossed a flake of hay into the feeder and checked the water level, dusting off her dress in the process.

"This is our last night together," Jax said as they walked out of the barn and headed toward the house.

"Yeah. I know."

Silence flowed between them for a few seconds until Jax continued. "I don't expect we'll get the chance to be alone again, but can I at least dance with you?"

"I'd like that." She said nothing else until they reached the house. What could she say? Her summer fling had turned into something more. The thought of going home to New York no longer appealed to her. What did she have back home? A growing career, good friends, the independence she'd searched for all her life.

Yet all of that seemed dark, pointless. Not when she would rather ride the trails with Jax.

But that was just silly fantasies. She had to think about her future and everything she'd worked for.

She walked past the lines of cars and into the clearing beyond the house where the crew had spent the day setting up for the party. The gentle clink and mumble of quiet conversation mixed with the soft music played in the background. They entered the staging area for the next contest, which Carl had explained earlier. They were to secure a charity donation from the wealthy guests who visited.

It's not like it wasn't something she'd done before.

The tasks had been outlined to them prior to the party, but Emmy had only half listened. Instead, she'd watched as her mother stood center stage and all but took over the show. After that, Emmy had escaped outside only to see her dad pull up in his truck.

At the party, the guests all wore formal gowns and suits, with the occasional cowboy boots thrown in. Some of them a bit more fancy than others, and several obvious marks for the contestants battling to secure the biggest donation.

The party was in full swing and contestants all flitted about smiling and laughing with guests, but her mother and father were nowhere to be seen. Jax crooked his elbow toward her, and she looped her arm through, enjoying the easy way she felt with him.

"Shall we schmooze our way into some charity money?"

She shook her head, but said, "I suppose. I've never liked this part of my mom's parties. They're never really about charity."

"You've done this before."

"Yep."

"Good. You can show me how." Jax made a wide berth around the crowd, searching the patrons for the perfect mark.

A few seconds in, Emmy spotted one of her mom's old

acquaintances who she knew had wide pockets. She lifted her chin toward him. "Over there. By the bar."

Jax nodded and eased them toward the man.

"Mr. Templeton," Emmy greeted, as though they were old friends.

"Emmy Wilson? Is that you?"

"It's been too long." She extended her hand out daintily, and he kissed her knuckles. "How is the wife? I believe you were on your third one the last time I saw you." Emmy settled her hip against the bar as Jax ordered them two drinks.

Thank God. She'd need a vodka or two to get her through tonight.

"Ah, yes, Jennifer." He nodded but smiled. "She's in the Turks and Caicos with her fifth husband, I believe."

"I'm sorry to hear that." Emmy turned to Jax. "Can I introduce you to Jax McCall? If it wasn't for him, we wouldn't have this wonderful little project."

"Mr. McCall." He shook Jax's hand. "I met your father earlier, I believe. Hard man."

Jax chuckled and reached out to grab their drinks from the bartender. "Yes, he is, sir."

"So Mr. Templeton. Don't tell me one of these other contestants has already won your donation?"

"One of the High Heel gals came up to talk to me earlier, but she didn't even ask." He searched the crowd, and after a moment turned back to Emmy. "What cause is Rochelle advocating for now?"

"This one is Stacy Siepres, I believe," Jax supplied. "And I think she said earlier today that it was to fight global warming or some such thing."

"Can't have those ice caps melting."

"True, but I don't know how flying a bunch of people out here to deprive them of their money will stop mother nature from turning on the heat every once in a while." Jax took a sip of his drink.

"I think what he means by that is Stacy has become very active in the fight against pollution and its effects on the earth's atmosphere."

"No, I didn't." Jax looked at her like she'd grown another head, but Mr. Templeton just chuckled.

"I don't see the point of it all either, my boy." Templeton took out a checkbook and pen from his inside jacket. "You were straight with me, so I'll be straight with you. I know this whole thing is a sham for this game show, but I like you." He scribbled out a check and handed it to Jax.

"Thank you, sir." Jax pocketed the check without even looking at the number.

"Now, Ms. Wilson. Tara Smithson over there is all about the global warming stuff, and she just got here. Go hit her up before any of these other kids can."

"Thank you, sir."

"And tell your mother I said hi, and that I'll expect her to make an appearance at my new wife's birthday party in September."

"Will do, sir."

Mr. Templeton meandered into the crowd and Emmy sucked down her drink, using the booze to ease the beat of her heart. She hated this part of networking events. Socializing. Schmoozing. She was no good at it.

"Come on, Bobcat. Let's go get you a donation."

For the next thirty minutes, she and Jax made the rounds of the crowd until she'd secured her donation. After which she let the minutes tick by in happy comfort until a murmur erupted from the crowd, followed by the thump of someone preparing a microphone.

"Excuse me," Stacy stepped up to the microphone. She waited for the crowd to silence before continuing, "Thank you all for coming tonight. First, I'd like to ask the contestants to place your donations in the donation box up here at the front table by the end of the party. We've had a wonderful few weeks filming the preview for High Heels and Cowboy Boots. I have a confession to make, though. This show is not what you thought it was. It's not a game show about cowboys and rich kids competing against each other. This is a show about how people from different worlds can work together to accomplish something great. It is the brainchild of me and my mentor, Ms. Rochelle Wilson."

Stacy clapped and stepped back from the microphone as Emmy's mother took her position. Right on cue to steal the spotlight. As always.

"Thank you, my dear." Emmy's mother hugged Stacy warmly. "High Heels and Cowboy Boots. As many of you know, Stacy is my neighbor and a dear, dear friend. She's been like the daughter I've always wanted."

"Well, that's a kick in the teeth," Emmy mumbled.

Jax leaned over to whisper in her ear. "Sorry, Bobcat."

"Eh. I'm used to it." And she was. She learned a long time ago not to take what her mother said to heart.

"As many of you know, my real daughter Emmy Wilson has been a constant in my life. She's been my rock." Her mom conjured up tears she knew were fake. "What you don't know, but what many have speculated on is who her father is." Her mother pointed to a reporter standing on the edge of the crowd, next to a cameraman. "Bob, I'm talking about you. The President of Turkmenistan, really?"

The crowd snickered and Bob raised one finger in recognition of her quip.

Rochelle faced the crowd once more, and Emmy knew what was coming next. Although she wasn't sure if she was excited about it, or nervous that the world she once knew was now about to change.

"I can confirm that The President of Turkmenistan is not Emmy's father." The crowd chuckled. "In fact, Emmy's father is a man whom I have battled with loving for years."

"No, she hasn't," Emmy mumbled under her breath.

"He wasn't the man I thought I wanted, but now I know he is the man I need. I've kept him a secret as we navigated an on again off again romance. I didn't want him caught up in the tabloid gossip." She eyed Bob the reporter again. "You can't blame me for that one, Bob." She winked. "So, without further ado, I'd like to introduce you to the love of my life, three-time National Finals Rodeo Saddle Bronc Champion, Tye Travers." She extended her hand to the side of the stage. "Tye?"

The crowd erupted in cheers and murmurs, but all Emmy could concentrate on was Jax as he shifted next to her.

He leaned in. "Why didn't you tell me Tye Travers was actually your dad?"

"I wasn't allowed to tell anyone. Plus, my mom is lying. They had no sort of real relationship. This is all a publicity stunt."

"You've never told anyone?" He stared at her in disbelief. "Not a single person your entire life?"

"No. I told one person." She chewed on her lower lip for a second. "Stacy."

"Stacy Siepres?" He sounded more hurt than anything else. "You trusted her, but you didn't think you could trust me?"

"I was like ten when I told her, and I thought she was my best friend at the time." Emmy scoffed. "My only friend, more like."

"I'm a fool. I guess I just liked you a little more than you did me." He yanked the donation check from his pocket. "Ever since high school."

"You can't seriously be pissed at me for not telling you something that they swore me to secrecy about?"

"Why not? You got pissed at me for God knows what on that mountain and left me to walk down alone at night." Jax gave her look of disgust. "Trust is something that matters in life. Even if we've only just discovered something that we could have."

Was he really this upset? Why? "Jax. Be realistic—"

"Emmy!" Stacy flounced up to her and tugged on her arm. "Come on stage. Your mom wants to show how loving your family is."

Emmy turned to Jax, but he'd already disappeared into the crowd as Stacy tugged her toward the stage. Her old neighbor had on a simple, sensible dress that hugged her curves but flowed to the grass. Not a nipple was showing. The silk material shined in the sparkling lights above head.

The perfect example of a High Heel. Everything Emmy wasn't and didn't want to be.

Emmy searched over the heads of the crowd, but if Jax was still here, he didn't want her to find him. But she had to. She hadn't expected him to react the way he did about her secret. Why did he care so much whether or not she'd lied to him?

Did he care for her more than she'd thought? Did he love her? She didn't even get to dance with him.

## CHAPTER 8

*J*ax scooted up until his groin pressed against the swell of his saddle. He closed his eyes for a moment to get the feel of the animal. It was something he always did, but that the rest of the guys gave him crap for. Problem was, every time he closed his eyes, all he saw was Emmy.

"You're gonna want to choke the bronc rein with this one," one of his buddies called out to him as he leaned over the chute.

"He has a tendency to kick out hard when he switches leads," another cowboy shouted. "Keep centered."

Adrenaline coursed through Jax, causing his hands to grow numb beneath the course line of the bronc rein. He jiggled his spurs, hooking them as far up on the horse's shoulder as he could to anchor himself to the mount, readied his position, and nodded.

The chute flew open at the same time the horse exploded from the tight confines. Jax jerked back as the horse lunged, dragging his hand behind his head to help him keep balance. As the horse planted his back feet on the ground once more,

Jax dragged his feet behind him to spur the back of his saddle, and then leaned back again to spur the horse's neck near the mane.

He struggled to keep his breath even as he moved his hips and adjusted his seat in time with the horse. Seconds ticked by like hours and every muscle in his body screamed at him to give in, let go and jump off. But he couldn't.

He continued like this, concentrating on the drag of his spurs along the horse and the way the rhythm of the animal flowed. Like a dance. Only this one was a little more painful than the one he didn't get to share with Emmy.

But he couldn't think of that now. He had to concentrate on the ride. He studied the horse's head and anticipated his next move, only instead of floating left like he'd expected, the mount jerked right and Jax almost lost his seat.

He used the pressure of his spurs and jerked his hand overhead to help him center once more on the saddle. Somewhere in the distance the buzzer sounded.

Jax waited for the peak of the next buck and then used the force of it to propel from the saddle, landing straight on his shoulder as he skidded to a stop in the arena.

Pain shot like a bullet from his shoulder all the way up his neck and back down the side of his body. He couldn't let anyone see, though. He was a cowboy. The only time he'd almost let himself show emotion was when he realized he'd fallen in love with Emmy Wilson. If she'd felt the same, she would have told him that his favorite saddle bronc rider wasn't just her godfather, but her dad.

It wasn't that she'd lied to him. It's what the lie meant. She didn't love him the way he did her. So he'd left the party and headed for the barn to help the hands feed the animals. It was after he'd finished that he'd bumped into Tye himself, who'd come to check on the horse Jax had bought from him, the one that would raise the price of his stock and help bring their ranch out of financial strain.

He'd talked to the man who'd raised Emmy, heard how he and her mother had patched things up, and how Rochelle was trying to break out Stacy's career while helping her own. He hadn't seemed impressed by the plan, but if it meant finally being able to claim his daughter, he'd go along.

Then he mentioned how happy Emmy was in her new job, making something of herself in New York, and all Jax could think about was how what they had wasn't meant to be. So he'd tracked down Chase and convinced him to leave for the rodeo before the sun rose the next morning. Like the coward he was, he ran away instead of telling Emmy the truth. He loved her. With all of his heart.

His dad had been pissed that he was leaving before the crew that day, of course, but it wasn't like he'd asked again to use his roping horse. Chase was still trying to scrounge up a better horse for him to ride than the inexperienced one he'd brought.

Jax stood and plucked his cowboy hat off the ground, slapping it against his thigh to shake the dirt. In the distance, past the rush of blood in his ears, the crowd shouted, cheering for him and his ride. The judge called out his number, but Jax didn't hear. All he could concentrate on was Emmy. Standing just outside the gate where a spectator shouldn't be. Not that it mattered to him.

She was here.

He approached the gate as a nearby cowboy opened it for him, and he walked out.

"I think you won this with that score," she said when he stopped in front of her.

He ran his gaze over her body. Unlike at the ranch when she'd mostly worn stylish clothes and ridiculous heels, she stood now in a pair of Justin's and a tight pair of jeans. Just as he'd seen her at the high school rodeos that season before she'd left him on the mountain. "You're wearing shoes today I see."

She wiggled one foot. "I had to drive all the way down here. I may ride barefoot, but I don't drive that way."

"You drove?"

"Yeah. With my dad." She motioned to the back of the fairgrounds where the trailers were parked. "Your dad said you needed a roping horse, so we stopped by my dad's place and grabbed Miles."

"Your dad's horse?"

"Don't worry, dad's been roping his local rodeos. You're the heeler, right?"

"Yes, but you didn't have to lend me your dad's horse."

"Once I sent the article that my mother and Stacy wanted me to write to my editor, and explained to him I think I was falling for you, he wanted to help. I've never had a real boyfriend before, and never dated a cowboy." Emmy took a step closer and lowered her voice. "But I honestly think he just wanted to feel like he was back in the game again. For real and not just the county fair."

"But... you came here? To me."

"I had to. You left without letting me explain."

"Explain what?"

"I didn't have a choice. I couldn't tell you who my dad was. I couldn't tell anyone my whole life. I wanted to... especially when we were in the meadow. But I couldn't. There's one thing my mom's lawyer is good at, and that's keeping people quiet. Legally. Why else would my father let her force him to claim me as a goddaughter and not his kid?"

"Your mom is..." he searched for a word that wouldn't insult her. "Determined."

"She's a meddling, selfish bitch, but I still love her." Emmy took a single step closer. "But that's not what I came here to talk about. I like you. I want to give us a shot. I still got a free vacation. We can go somewhere," she joked.

He took a deep breath and rubbed his hand across his mouth. "What about New York? Long distances don't work."

"We'll make it work. At least initially. I have a job there, but giving us a shot is more important. I can probably find a remote writing job or maybe even one in Montana." She chuckled sarcastically. "Or who knows, maybe I'll jump in and be the star of Stacy's actual reality show."

"I doubt that." Jax half-smiled. "The only star of Stacy's reality show is going to be Stacy."

"We'll figure it out." Emmy lowered her eyelashes as she spoke. "The point is, I want to be with you. I want us to work. If you'll have me?"

"Woman," he scooped her up in his arms, not caring one whit that he'd just soiled her clothes with arena dirt and probably something a little more grotesque. She was his. The woman he couldn't get out of his mind. "You stole my heart when you stole my truck. I've wanted you since then."

"You're every woman's fantasy." She snuggled deeper into his embrace. "Especially my friend Marissa's. She's going to be pissed when she learns that I've fallen in love with a cowboy."

"You'll have to bring her over sometime. Chase could use a good girl." He cupped her jaw in his hands and bent down to taste her sweet lips. The perfect mixture of everything that was Emmy—sweet and salty with just a hint of sin.

His woman in high heels and cowboy boots.

## SNEAK PEEK (BOOK 2): BLUE JEANS AND BUBBLE BATHS

"*H*ow often do people get kidnapped and murdered from the middle of nowhere? Are there even statistics on that?" Marissa Martinez asked her best friend as she turned down the lonely dirt road leading to Emmy's new home. Of course, Emmy was stuck somewhere between Cheyenne and the Montana border after having blown a transmission on her moving truck, but at least Marissa had her on speaker as she navigated this backwoods town.

"No one has ever been murdered in Willow Springs," her friend reassured.

"That you know of." Marissa bit her lip when Emmy muffled her end of the phone, drowning out some background noise and whatever it was her friend was saying to someone nearby.

"Emmy... Emmy." She called to draw her friend's attention once more, her heart beating with each rut she took just a little too fast. "This is the first time I've ever gone down a dirt road."

"Just take it slow." Emmy said, briefly unmuffling the phone.

Marissa slowed a bit, and her heartbeat returned to normal. "Are you sure it's okay if I stay in the house without you? I can get a hotel and wait for you and Jax to make it here." Marissa scanned her rearview mirror, but all she saw was dust. "Well, actually... is there even a hotel in this town? The only thing I saw in was a bar and a gas station."

Emmy unmuffled the phone and the background noise kicked up once more. "There is a hotel half of a mile out of the town other way, but you don't want to stay there. Trust me. Make yourself at home. If the door's locked then just keep going on the dirt road until you get to a fork. Take the left fork until you see a sign that says Chisum Ranch. Ask for Chase. He'll let you in the house."

"Do cowboys not use cell phones?"

"Sometimes cell signal is spotty out there so it'll be easier to just go get him, but he's been house-sitting. He was supposed to leave the door unlocked and keys on the counter for us. So it should be open."

Marissa pulled into the driveway—if you could call it that —and sighed. "Please don't tell me you've traded in your New York flat to become trailer trash?"

"Who are you calling trash? I'll have you know, that is a double wide. Not some RV on a lot."

"It's a trailer." She raised both eyebrows as she spoke, not that Emmy could see her.

"It's got a jet tub in the master bath just off the living room. It's perfect. You should take a bath. Get the road grime off. It's amazing."

She studied the numbers on the side of the double-wide. "2589 Lone Tree Trail, right?"

"That's it." Her friend muffled the noises again and said something to someone.

"Emmy?" She knew her friend was busy with the repair shop, but she couldn't help but need the extra support as she navigated what was sure to be the smallest town she'd ever been through. And it made her nervous. She was a city girl. She could ride the subway with someone urinating in the corner in total comfort, but not seeing a single person for over thirty minutes scared the hell out of her.

"Sorry. Jax is talking to the repair guy about the truck. Looks like it will be a few days."

"A few days?" Marissa sighed, shut down the car, and stepped out to slam the door. She would do this alone. For the first time in her life, she'd left the city. She'd been okay with it until she had to go on without her best friend and only moral support. She could do this. She had to. She was already here. "I'm gonna check the door. Stay on the phone in case I need those directions again."

"Okay," Emmy answered, and muffled the phone.

Marissa picked her way across the dirt in her red high-heeled cowboy boots and mini skirt—an outfit she picked out just in case she came across any cowboys on her way through town. Which she didn't. Not that it would have done her any good. Before she'd left New York, she'd sworn off men—after a failed relationship with a guy she'd met in a coffee shop.

She frowned at her own self promise. Too bad. She'd been in love with the thought of a hot cowboy ever since Emmy dragged her to her first PBR event in Madison Square Garden. But she was done with them. She had to be. For her own sake.

She climbed the stairs and turned the knob; only to freeze as a buzzing sound penetrated her thoughts and made her fingers grow cold. She slowly lifted her gaze to the beehive suspended in the corner of the door frame.

"Oh. My. God. Emmy," she hissed the words as fear slid through her veins. Her breath froze in her chest as a bee dove straight at her. She ducked and let out a slight squeal.

"What?" Emmy asked. Marissa didn't answer, but ducked another attack. Emmy snapped, "What is it, Marissa?"

"Beeeees," Marissa screeched as another dove at her. She ducked to the right as the bee flew straight into the back of her shirt. Her heart raced as she screamed and rushed through the door.

Emmy said something on the other end of the receiver, but she couldn't understand, and didn't care. As fast as she could, she ran through the living room, stripping her shirt over her head. She somehow got her shirt off before getting stung, but the dammed bee charged at her again, more angry than before. She ran into the closest room, clutching her phone in one hand and shirt in the other.

Just as Emmy had said, she'd made it to the master bedroom. On the other side of the room stood a bathroom, so she headed inside, using her shirt to slap the air just in case the bee followed. She slammed the door just as the little ass hole charged at her again.

She slumped against the door in relief.

"Usually people knock, but if you're that desperate for a bubble bath, there's room enough for two in here," a deep male voice sounded somewhere in the bathroom. "Although, you have to take off the rest of your clothes."

Marissa had never squeaked so much in her life, but here she was letting out a little mouse sound as she met eyes with a cowboy in the jet tub. At least she assumed he was a cowboy by the way he sported the farmers tan, hat hair, and well-defined muscles.

"Sorry. Didn't mean to scare you," he said at her sound. "Then again, you're on the trespassing in someone else's house." He laid his head back and closed his eyes. "Maybe I should call the cops."

It took a few seconds for her to regain her composure.

Mostly. The man seemed to heat the already steamy bathroom up even more, causing the world around her to fog, except for the sight of him in the tub.

She stood up straight, regaining her composure. "You aren't reacting like someone who is worried about a trespasser."

"Sweetheart, I just came off a horse. Flew over his head and landed on my shoulder. I'm not about to injure it more by overreacting to a pretty girl coming into my buddy's house like she was running from something." He opened one eye and looked at her. "Bees getcha?" On her nod, he closed his eye again and relaxed. "Sorry. That's my fault. I haven't gotten around to knocking it down yet. And I figure if you're this far out of town, then you didn't find this house by accident. I'm just glad you're not Emmy."

"Maybe I should call the cops. I'm Marissa. You're the one trespassing in my friend's house."

"Spunky. I like that." He turned his head to watch her once more. "Name's Chase. So now that we're acquainted, either finish undressing and hop in, or close the door on your way out."

Only then did she realize she stood there in nothing but her miniskirt, bra, and designer boots. She dropped her phone onto the counter and, shaking her shirt out just in case, she jerked it over her head.

He frowned. "Too bad. You look like you'd be fun to take a bath with."

Oh Good Lord, he was smooth. Exactly what she'd imagined he'd be like every time Emmy had talked about him. The perfect cowboy. Too bad she met him right after going celibate.

WITHOUT A CARE to the water dripping over the side and

onto the floor, Chase reached out to side of the tub with his good arm and grabbed his beer, taking a long swig. His move was more smooth and cool than the way he felt inside. The woman before him twisted his gut into a honda knot with her dark hair and perfectly formed breasts. All packaged neatly beneath her pink, lace bra—the only thing she wore besides her skirt and boots.

Holy shit, she was hot!

He'd heard her outside screeching when the bees came at her, but his shoulder hurt like hell. He needed a good soak.

As far as he knew, Emmy and her group of travelers were staying behind in Wyoming to get the truck fixed. He hadn't expected one of them to come ahead of the rest. Plus, he didn't expect her to bust in. He thought whoever was out there would have knocked if they got past the bees. And not knowing who it was at the door, he'd planned to ignore the visitor.

He was glad she'd busted in, though. When he saw her run into the bathroom, he knew it was Emmy's friend. He'd seen pictures. Although pictures didn't do her justice.

The woman was stunning. Not like any of the women they had around here. Marissa was soft and curvy. The designer clothes she wore—right down to her ridiculous red cowboy boots, if you can call them that—made him hard the moment she walked in. He was just glad he had bubbles to hide his erection.

Of course, she wasn't wearing a shirt and her breasts looked like they wanted to break free of her black lace bra. Those two things, combined with the skirt he'd wanted to hike up just a little to see that thigh tattoo peeking out every once in a while, proved she belonged more in the concrete jungle than the dusty country roads of Montana.

Man, he was done for.

But he was relaxed. Calm. Unaffected. Right?

Needing the cool of the beer in his throat, he took another long drag and focused his gaze on the bubble that had stuck to the wall bedside the tub. He carefully rested his injured arm along the edge, stealing his calm from the giant tub. He'd gotten pills from the doctor after he'd set it following the dislocation, but who needed those when you had beer.

And bubble baths.

His elbow brushed the bottle of lavender-scented soap he'd stolen from his mom before coming over here. He cringe inwardly and resisted the urge to hide it from Marissa —the woman his friend's fiancé had talked about so much that he was sure she'd planned to set them up.

But the soap could be Emmy's, right?

Yep. Let's go with that.

God he was a blundering fool right now. At least he wasn't blundering out loud. Then again, the silence had stretched long enough to make it awkward.

He cleared his throat to fill the silence.

From deep within Marissa's cellphone, Emmy's tiny voice echoed through the bathroom. "Is that Chase? Is he in the tub again?"

"Emmy?" His heart palpitated. Damn it! His calm wavered, and he sat upright out of reflex, careful not to expose his boys to the dark-haired beauty before him. "Hey. Emmy. I thought you were stuck in Cheyenne."

"Oh, my, God. Put me on speaker," Emmy's voice echoed.

Marissa gave a 'you're done for now' smile and did as directed.

"Chase Chisum," Emmy began. "I told you before we left to stay out of my tub."

"Sorry, Em. I wasn't in here long. I broke a mare today and landed on my shoulder."

"Yeah I heard," Emmy snapped.

Marissa flipped her gaze to the lavender soap. "Don't believe him, Emmy. He's used all of your body wash for bubbles or he's normally a pretty smelling man. Lavender smells like." Chase's heart began to beat hard when the spunky woman reached down and dipped four perfectly manicured fingers into his bathwater, coming just inches from brushing his hip with her fingertips. She pouted her lips just a little. "The water is almost cold. I'd say he's been in here at least an hour." Marissa lowered the phone and directed the next comment at him. "Shouldn't the bubbles be gone by now?"

Calling forth some playboy cool he normally sported, he gave what he hoped was a crooked smile. "I refreshed."

God, this woman was intoxicating.

Out of sheer need to take control of the situation, he reached up and clasped her wrist when she pulled her hand away from his water. "Don't start a war you can't finish, Sweetheart. I'm not against pulling a pretty girl in here with me just to get my revenge."

"You don't even know me." She raised a single brow, but beneath his fingers her heartbeat raced. That small bit of knowledge eased his own nerves. He grinned right back at her.

"So, Ms. Marissa," he drawled. "Emmy has told me enough to pique my interest. You ratted me out. You deserve to be… wet." He smiled and slid his gaze down to her cleavage, peeking out from the neck of her low cut shirt as she bent over the tub.

"Knock it off, Chase." Emmy called from her phone. "Let my friend go. Get out of my tub and get your clothes on or else Jax says he's kicking your ass the moment he gets in to town."

Chase sighed. "Fine."

He released his grip on Marissa's wrist, but it took her a

second to regain her composure and stand up straight. He tried not to gloat when she lifted her chin just a little higher as a spark flashed across her eyes.

He smirked and tilted his head to the side. "I'd stand, but I don't want to tempt you to take that bath you said you don't want."

"I… I'll…" she shook her head as if trying to rattle around the words to form a sentence.

Instead, she shook her head and left the bathroom, grabbing her phone before she shut the door.

Chase stepped from the tub and wrapped a towel around his hips.

Marissa must have wandered a few steps into the room, but didn't count on how thin the walls were because he could still hear her and Emmy's muffled voices.

"What the hell, Emmy? You never said Chase was hot."

"Oh, my gosh, Marissa. Get ahold of yourself. There are plenty of cowboys in town looking for a girl just like you. And most of them will be at the wedding. Pace yourself."

"But Chase is…" Marissa paused. "Chase is all of my Urban Cowboys plus the ones I see on TV all dipped into one hot-ass bathtub."

"So help me, if you have sex in my bed, I'll kill you."

Chase let himself drip dry for a few minutes, not wanting to interrupt this very interesting conversation.

"Who do you think I am? I wouldn't do that with your future husband's best friend… no matter how tempting it might be. Don't worry. I'm the kinda girl that makes a man work for it."

"Unless they give you a whiskey and show you their belt buckle."

Chase tipped his mouth up in a half-grin at the little tidbit of information. This was getting good, but he felt like a creep listening at the door the way he was. But he prided himself on being anything but.

"So that's all it takes?" Chase asked, walking out of the bathroom, hoping to shake her just a little. "Well, hell, I got one right here."

Marissa turned, her eyes widened as he caught her gaze and held it while he made his way across the living room toward the guest room he'd been staying in. The place where'd left his clothes. Within seconds, he returned and held it out to her.

This was a cocky move on his part, but he was having fun, and maybe testing the waters just a little. Hoping they weren't as cold as his bath had been when she'd dipped her fingers in and scorched his insides. "My buckle is the real deal, though. This one is from the Cheyenne rodeo, but I have one from the National Finals Rodeo if that's what gets you going."

Was she impressed by a shiny piece of metal? He mentally shrugged. Some girls were. Was she one of them?

"You're a pig."

Nope. Not impressed.

"Thin walls." He winked.

"Hey, Marissa," Emmy called from the phone. "I don't have lavender soap."

Half embarrassed and half cocky, he held Marissa's gaze, reached out and grabbed the phone from her hand. Now he had to own to it. Without breaking eye contact with her, he held the phone up between them. "Emmy, your friend will have to call you back."

Emmy protested, but he pressed the button and hung up, blocking out all sound except the rush of blood past her ears.

He should step away from her a bit. Give her space. Except the closer he got, the more he could see the little lines on her lips and all he could think about was the way they would feel pressed against his. Urging her mouth to open up to him. Making their way down her body toward her...

Get a grip, Chase! Leave her alone. She's Emmy's friend, not some buckle bunny.

She reached out and caressed the shiny silver oval with a cowboy figure roping a steer, etched in gold in the center. Causing him to grow hard. He twitched backward just a little, needing to hide the effect she had on him.

She sidled closer, but the look in her eye warned him. She was playing. Calling his bluff. She brushed her breasts against his arm, just a little. "So you're like a real cowboy."

He ticked his chin to the side slightly as the vein at the base of his neck thumped. He knew she was toying with him, but damn it, he couldn't back away. "That's right. The real deal."

"Is it true cowboys only stay on for eight seconds?"

He smiled, trying to remain cool. "That's bull riders. I'm a team roper."

"Oh, a team roper." She stepped away from him. "The bubble bath makes sense now."

That cooled him down a bit. "Good Lord, no, woman. It's where two people rope a steer. It's an actual skill needed on the ranch."

She raised a single eyebrow seductively, dropping back into their sensual battle. "Mmm. So you can lasso me?"

This woman was going to kill him.

"And hog tie you," he supplied, hoping to regain some kind of upper hand. His skin tingled with the need for her to touch him again. She had to know what she was doing to him. "If that's what you're into."

"I like all kinds of things." She satisfied his silent craving, walking her fingers up his bare chest. His abs shuttered beneath her hand, and she smiled seductively. "You don't live here, right?"

"Nope. Just house sitting."

"Good." With a speed he didn't expect, she grabbed his belt away from him and stepped back. "I live here... for the time being. I'll expect you to be gone by the time I get done with my bath. Alone."

At that, she walked into the bedroom. The lock clicked behind her.

Relief and disappointment flooded his body. He'd never met a woman like her. This woman from the city might just be his undoing.

## ABOUT THE AUTHOR

A country girl born and bred, **Dawn Luedecke** has spent most of her life surrounded by horses, country folk, and the wild terrain of Nevada, Idaho and Montana. After high school she joined the Coast Guard where she met and married her very own alpha male and drill instructor. She enjoys writing historical and contemporary romance and spends as much time as she can working on her current manuscript. For more information visit: www.dawn-luedeckebooks.com.

facebook.com/authordawnluedecke

twitter.com/d_luedecke

instagram.com/dawnluedeckebooks

amazon.com/author/dawnluedecke

bookbub.com/authors/dawn-luedecke

goodreads.com/dawnluedecke

pinterest.com/dluedecke

## JOIN MY NEWSLETTER

Want to be the first to know when Dawn has a new release? How about giveaways, events, and other fun stuff? Visit www.dawnluedeckebooks.com to sign up or click the image below to sign up for Dawn's newsletter.

## FULL LENGTH CONTEMPORARY

### The Hard Corps Romance Series

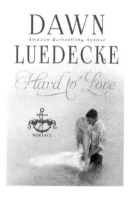

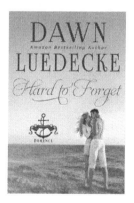

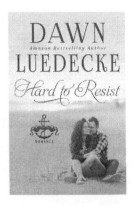

**Short Story Contemporary**

HISTORICAL ROMANCE

**The Montana Girl Series**

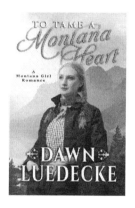

## The Montana Mountain Series

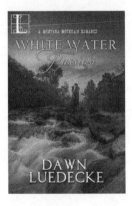

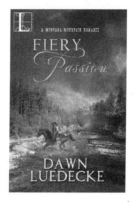

HISTORICAL SHORT STORIES

**The Lighthouse Romance Anthology**

**Featuring all 4 books in the Life Saving Series**

**The Life Saving Series**

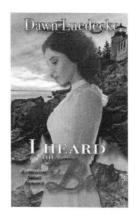

THANK YOU FOR READING HIGH
HEELS AND COWBOY BOOTS: A
LONE TREE RANCH ROMANCE

Made in the USA
Columbia, SC
28 November 2020

25723111R00086